Discovery at Béal na Bláth

Written by Joel Ring

Cover Art and Layout by James Ring

I would like to thank my wonderful wife Susie and my son James for their unwavering encouragement to bring this book to fruition. I would also like to thank Linda Tucker of Cup and Quill Editing for all their professional advice.

The idea for this story came after a family trip to Ireland. There we met wonderfully friendly people and learned of Irish history.

Most importantly, I would like to say this fictional adventure story is by no means intended to make light of the struggles and hardships endured by the brave men and women who fought for Ireland's independence.

I hope you enjoy the adventure.

Joel Ring

Table of Contents

Discovery at
Béal na Bláth

"If the Big Fellow says we're goin', we're goin'," Vinny Byrne tells Emmett Dalton.

"But it doesn't make any sense to go to Cork now," sighs Emmett. Dalton and Byrne are two of Michael Collins's most trusted "Apostles."

Michael Collins and Éamon de Valera are veterans of the 1916 Easter Rising. After that attempt at Irish independence failed, they were imprisoned by the British. They were released after two years due to pressure from the United States on Britain's treatment of the Irish. From 1919 to 1921, de Valera, nicknamed "The Long Fellow" due to his lanky stature, was in America raising funds for the cause of Irish independence. Michael Collins, nicknamed "the Big Fellow" due to his tall, athletic build, was in Dublin. He is Head of Intelligence in the newly formed Irish Republican Army, the IRA. The IRA is perpetuating a guerrilla war against the occupying British troops to gain Ireland's independence.

Collins has recruited a band of twelve young men, all twenty to twenty-four years of age, unmarried, and who have no qualms about taking human life in the name of Irish independence. This special unit of assassins is nicknamed "the Apostles." Together, under Collin's leadership, they carry out assassinations and bombings against the agents of the Crown occupying Ireland. This action helps bring the British Empire to the bargaining table for peace. The British Prime Minister at this time is Sir David Lloyd George, "the Welsh Wizard."

It's August 1922. Ireland has devolved into a civil war. The internal strife started when Collins and a delegation of plenipotentiaries returned from London. They have negotiated a treaty to end Anglo-Irish hostilities. The treaty states that all British military and police will be removed from Ireland, thus creating a Free State with self-rule and policing but no republic. The treaty makes Ireland a Free State *within* the British Empire. Its elected leaders must swear an oath of allegiance to the King of England. The major caveat in the treaty is that Ulster, the six counties in the predominantly Protestant-controlled North, will remain under British rule. This causes a seismic rift in the IRA. Collins sees that a republic was never on the table at negotiations. Britain would not even consider it. He sees this treaty as the best deal they can get to free the Irish from under the British yoke. He also sees it as a pathway to an eventual republic.

De Valera, president of the Irish "Republic," knows England will never agree to a republic. He does not attend the negotiations in London. When Collins returns from London with the treaty, the Dáil Éireann—the unicameral parliament of the Irish Republic—ratifies the treaty by a narrow majority. Until the treaty vote, it refused to recognize the British Parliament at Westminster. Instead, it saw itself as the independent legislature of Ireland. The Dáil ratifies the treaty to end hostilities and become a Free State within the British Empire, realizing this is the best and first step toward a republic. De Valera and his followers resign from the Dáil. De Valera knows this is the best deal England will allow but resigns over the idealistic view of a "Republic or nothing." This action causes a split in the previously united IRA, and de Valera and his Republicans go to war with the newly formed Free State Army, led by Collins. It is not a realistic cause, but they are willing to die for their ideals.

"The Big Fellow says he has an important meeting in Farnes, West Cork, that can change everything," Vinny Byrne replies.

CHAPTER 2
BÉAL NA BLÁTH, IRELAND
2023

"Don't you just love waking up here?" Mary stretches and yawns in bed. "Don't touch me; you'll ruin it," she says, her arms over her head, toes pointing southward. Dorian is always hugging her mid-stretch and "ruining it."

"I'm just happy waking up next to you," says Dorian, reaching for her.

They have been married for thirty-seven years. Mary had been a registered oncology nurse, and Dorian was a union ironworker. That's all behind them now. They are expatriates living on a couple of acres in green old Ireland. They have three children, all grown. Christian lives in Switzerland, Patrick lives in Australia, and Grace, their youngest, lives in Ireland. Grace just started her new job in Killarney in the Kerry County Medical Examiner Office.

"What would you like for breakfast? I'll go make the coffee," yells Dorian a few minutes later from the bathroom.

"Just a hard-boiled egg for me, and I'll pick at yours," replies Mary, getting out of bed.

"How do you know what I'm having?" says Dorian playfully.

"Bacon, sausage, eggs, and toast, same as every breakfast

you've made since we moved here." Mary laughs.

Dorian heads downstairs. Sundance, their new white Labrador Retriever puppy, follows behind, his tail wagging as he bounds down the steps. The pup already knows the routine. If he follows Dorian, there is a good chance there will be people food for him. Dorian makes the coffee. He goes into the refrigerator to retrieve the eggs, bacon, and sausages. Turning on the stovetop, he begins to cook. Sundance sits at his feet.

Upstairs, Mary gets in the shower. Aromas of coffee and bacon are wafting up the stairs. She smiles to herself. What a lovely life they have made for themselves!

At breakfast, Mary says in a fake, stern voice, "Enough of that laying around all day reading spy novels! I'd like you to fix that wall out front. It's uneven, and you know how I like symmetry." She butters her toast and steals the last sausage off Dorian's plate. Dorian smiles as he scrapes the last of the egg yolk off his plate with the sourdough toast.

"Yeah, sure, symmetry," Dorian says sarcastically as he finishes his coffee, getting up from the table.

The sun is shining, drying up the last of the morning dew. Mary makes her way to the porch swing to settle in with her book on gardening. Dorian heads out front, surveying the wall. It is a fieldstone wall built with no mortar, like all the other fieldstone walls lining the roads in Ireland.

She's right, he thinks. *There is a low spot. It's about one-and-a-half feet lower than the rest of the wall.* Dorian goes around back to get his wheelbarrow. "The only wheelbarrow I've paid for," he mutters. Throughout his construction career, Dorian had a knack for "acquiring" certain hand tools and sometimes larger ones. Back in New Jersey, he'd had a garage full of shovels, rakes, picks, and wheelbarrows. He couldn't help himself; it was like an obsession.

While gathering the fieldstones from around the yard, Dorian gazes over at Mary, engrossed in her book. They were teenagers

when they met and started dating in Upper Creek. That was forty years and three children ago, but when he looks into her eyes, she's still fifteen to him. They are a perfect match. He is handsome, brutish, and sloppy. She is pretty, refined, and obsessively neat. Together, they fit like two opposite halves, making a perfect whole.

Gathering fieldstones from the property and piling them up by the low spot takes most of the morning. While dumping the wheelbarrow, Dorian notices a herd of sheep being led up the road.

You don't see this in Hudson County, he thinks. The sheep have blue spray paint marks on their necks. "I guess people 'acquire' sheep around here," he comments to himself. "Top of the morning!" he calls to the man following the sheep.

"And the rest of the day to you!" shouts the shepherd. Dorian chuckles as he waves.

"You want lunch?" Mary calls from the porch. "I made tuna."

"Yeah, sure, I'll be right in!" Dorian yells back. Putting the wheelbarrow behind the house, he thinks, *If they're worried about sheep acquirement, I'm not taking any chances.*

Once inside, he sees that Mary has a fine lunch set on the table. There is tuna salad on pumpernickel bread with heirloom tomatoes and lemonade.

"I'm so happy we did this." Mary sighs as they sit down to eat. Some years earlier, before they both retired, Dorian, Mary, and the children had a family vacation to Ireland. Mary fell in love with the place, and Dorian loved her. That's where the plan came from to retire here. When Grace, their youngest, landed a job at the Kerry County Medical Examiner's Office, that sealed the deal. They retired and sold their home, cars, tools, even the wheelbarrows. The only thing Dorian brought with him was his winemaking equipment.

They'd had a family vacation on the North Fork of Long Island twenty years earlier. Dorian took an interest in winemaking after seeing all the vineyards there. Every year, Dorian would have

grapes shipped from Napa, California. He bought a thirty-gallon American Oak barrel. This made 144 bottles of wine, usually pinot noir. Dorian and Mary would give them out to neighbors, friends, and work colleagues; you name it, they got a bottle of wine. It was a great source of joy for Dorian, so he shipped all his winemaking equipment to Ireland when they moved.

"This fall, I think I will buy the grapes from France. It's closer than Napa. What do you think?" asks Dorian, sitting down to eat.

"I think that's a great idea. You can get them from Burgundy." Mary smiles as she pulls in her chair. "Next week, I want you to plant a garden. I'd love to grow these," she says, pointing at the tomatoes. "The yard behind the house is so nice and level. You could build me some raised beds."

"Yeah, sure, whatever you want." Dorian finishes the last bite of his sandwich, then gulps down the lemonade.

"You eat like an animal! You don't even taste it, do you?" remarks Mary.

"Yeah, sure, I know, and if I did taste it, it was delicious." He smiles, rising from the table.

Back out in the yard, with all the new stones gathered, Dorian removes the top layer of stones from the low spot on the wall. He is removing the existing smaller stones to add new, bigger stones to the bottom and attain the proper height.

"Symmetry," he mumbles to himself as he labors. While removing old stones, he finds a hollow section in the wall. "That's weird," he says in his thick Hudson County accent. Dorian investigates further into the cavity. He spies the top of a bottle with a cork in it. Continuing to excavate the dirt and sediment gently, Dorian is able to dislodge the bottle without breaking it. It is an old, clear, quart-sized bottle. The label on it reads POWERS WHISKEY. Cleaning off the dirt, he notices a sheet of paper is rolled up inside. "Mary! Mary! I found McGuirk's treasure map!" he yells, heading

toward the house.

McGuirk was a fictional pirate Dorian had made up when the kids were little. He buried an old coffee can filled with silver dollars and fifty-cent pieces in the yard. He made a copy of the land survey and aged it by rubbing used tea bags over it and turning it into a treasure map. During their renovation, he made out that he had found it buried in the walls of the house. The kids were occupied for a week until they found the X that marked the spot. He makes his way into the kitchen. "Mary! Mary, look what I found!"

"Don't! You'll get mud everywhere!" she scolds, coming to the table.

"No, wait, there is something inside."

CHAPTER 3
LONDON, ENGLAND
DECEMBER 1921

"Do you really have to go back?" coos Hazel from under the down comforter.

Michael Collins is getting dressed. "What would Lloyd George think if I were to take up residency in London? Never mind your husband, darlin'," Collins says with a laugh while lacing up his shoes and sitting on the edge of the bed.

Lady Hazel Lavery is the wife of Sir John Lavery, a portrait painter who doesn't pay nearly enough attention to his social butterfly wife. Lady Hazel is in her midtwenties, tall and pretty. She has light brown hair that falls to her shoulders. The color of her eyes matches her name. She is infatuated with her "handsome bad boy," Michael Collins.

Collins is in London to head the Irish delegation and negotiate a peace accord with the British.

"Who knows?" Lady Hazel says, sitting up in the bed. "Lloyd George *is* rumored to have *tendencies*."

Collins stops and stands up. He is a master at working an intelligence network. Throughout Ireland and even here in London, he has informants. Using the information he receives from these spies, he dispatches his Apostles to carry out "jobs." Collins's efficacy in this brutal assassination business brought the British to the bargaining table.

"What?" Collins questions. "Can you get me evidence of these tendencies, darlin'?"

"My husband, John, paints portraits for most of London's elite. While sitting for their portrait, they love to gossip and speak in innuendo." Hazel gets out of bed and puts her robe on. "It seems the prime minister has a 'peculiar' relationship with Prince Henry, Duke of Gloucester."

"Jesus, love! Get me something concrete on that, and I'll have the old bugger at my mercy! Ireland will be free, all of Ireland!" His eyes twinkling, Collins puts his arms around Hazel and picks her off the floor, twirling her around. She wraps her arms around his neck and kisses him passionately.

CHAPTER 4
CROW STREET SAFE HOUSE, DUBLIN, IRELAND
APRIL 1922

Emmett Dalton walks up the flight of narrow wooden stairs. Opening the door, he finds Vinny Byrne sitting at a small rectangular table, sipping his coffee and finishing a pound of rashers and beans. "The Big Fellow would like to know if there is any correspondence from London today."

"I'll check the library this morning." Emmett is amazed at how much Byrne can eat. "My God, man! Do you eat every meal like it's going to be your last?" Emmett laughs.

"You do realize the line of work we are engaged in now, don't ya? Ya gobshite! Now, never mind my diet, and get to the library. The Big Fellow doesn't like procrastinators!" barks Byrne.

This is true. Michael Collins is maniacal about punctuality and efficiency. This is part of what makes his operation so successful. He has established drop-off points throughout the city. Porters, waiters, housemaids, bakers, and milkmen are his eyes and ears. He even has chambermaids in London's Royal Houses and lorry drivers who deliver supplies to the House of Commons working for him. They use libraries, bakeries, tailor shops, and the like to leave coded messages on any information they discover about British operations or personnel. This correspondence is collected and delivered to one of the safe houses all over Dublin. Collins spends his day bicycling from point to point, deciphering these messages. Then he formulates a plan and dispatches his Apostles to carry out the "job." It is a most deadly and efficient operation.

CHAPTER 5
REGENT STREET LONDON
JANUARY 1922

It's a bright, sunny day in London. Lady Hazel Lavery's driver drops her off on Regent Street. She is out shopping for the day. While waiting to cross the street in front of Robinson and Cleaver Department Store, she is approached by a woman selling scarves. Hazel tries to ignore the woman by not making eye contact.

"A hazel scarf for a lovely young Hazel?" The old woman says in an Irish brogue. The woman hands Lady Hazel the scarf and walks on down the street. Lady Hazel crosses the road to hurry away from the strange woman. Once on the other side of the street, she notices a small piece of paper attached to the scarf.

Hazel looks around. Not seeing anyone watching her or the odd woman, she enters the Robinson and Cleaver. Still bewildered by the note, Hazel picks out the first item she comes to, a pajama outfit, and heads to the dressing room. Once inside the fitting area, she closes the curtain and opens the note.

Darlin,

I have a contact in 10 Downing Street. She'll be in "touch" with you. Bring the film to Johnson Bakery Supply on Pettis St.

M. C.

Lady Hazel immediately shreds the note into little pieces and puts them in her purse. Bringing the pajama suit back, she asks the salesgirl, "Excuse me, where is the powder room?"

"Down the stairs to the right, milady," instructs the salesgirl. Lady Hazel descends the stairs and enters the powder room. She locks the door, puts the shredded pieces of the note into the toilet, and flushes them. Returning upstairs, she continues to shop.

CHAPTER 6
LAVERY MANSION, LONDON
JANUARY 1922

"John, dear!" Hazel Lavery walks into the parlor with a shopping bag. "Look what I purchased at Robinson and Cleaver on Regent Street."

"What now, lovey? A new pajama suit or another cloche hat?" Sir John questions dryly.

"No, silly! A camera!" Hazel pulls the camera from the shopping bag. "It's a Vest Pocket Autographic Kodak from America. It's the most recent model! Photography is the latest craze all over the continent."

John looks up from his newspaper. "Dearest, I make my living as a portrait painter. Do I look like I want to embrace photography?"

"Not for you, dear! I purchased the Kodak for me! You can paint them, and I will photograph them. It will all be such great fun!" Hazel laughs.

John rises from his chair and walks to his wife. "I have an appointment with the prime minister this afternoon. Sir Lloyd George would like to sit for his portrait. It will be hung in the House of Commons if he approves the likeness." Sir John leaves the parlor to pack his easel and paint supplies in his oversized satchel. Hazel chases after him.

"Oh, please let me accompany you! I haven't seen Sir George since Christmas time. He is such delightful company!" Hazel puts her arms around her husband's neck and begins kissing him.

"All right, you can join me," whispers John, nibbling Hazel's ear. Together, they retire to the bedroom.

It's late afternoon when the Laverys arrive at Sir Lloyd George's residence, 10 Downing Street. The butler answers the door and shows them into the parlor.

"Mr. Prime Minister? Sir John and Lady Hazel Lavery to see you," announces the butler.

"Yes, yes, show them in." Lloyd George rises from his chair by the fireplace to greet them.

"Sir John, come in. Lady Hazel, so lovely to see you again! What a pleasant surprise!" He reaches down, kissing her hand.

"Oh, Georgie! Such a gentleman!" Hazel says, sounding coy. Sir John sets up his easel and positions Lloyd George in front of the large floor-to-ceiling windows. Lady Hazel reclines in the oversized leather chair before the roaring fire.

In a short while, the maid, Annie Malone, enters the room with cucumber sandwiches and tea on a large silver serving platter for Lady Hazel while her husband is busy painting. Annie puts the tray on the hand-carved chestnut tea table. Annie discreetly taps the back of Hazel's hand and winks while making eye contact with Lady Hazel. Hazel picks up on the signal and nods subtly.

A half-hour later, Annie returns to clear the tray. Lady Hazel politely asks, "Excuse me, could you please show me the powder room?"

"Yes, my lady, right this way," replies Annie. Lady Hazel picks up her purse and follows Annie out of the room and down the hall.

Upon exiting the powder room, Lady Hazel finds Annie

waiting for her down the hall. Annie puts her finger to her lips, and together, they ascend the wide, curving mahogany staircase. Once on the second floor, Annie leads Lady Hazel down the upper hall to Lloyd George's bedroom. Entering the bedroom, Annie shuts the door behind them.

"You can hide in here," Annie says, pointing to a large Birdseye Maple armoire. The armoire has two doors; one side is solid and has drawers, and the other has a pane of beveled glass halfway up. That side has no drawers, just a rod to hang shirts and trousers. Opening the side with the glass, Annie removes a pair of pajamas and lays them on the bed. Annie then splits the remaining clothes hangers in half. Hazel takes off her shoes and removes the Kodak from her purse. She checks that the film is loaded properly and puts her shoes and bag in the armoire. Annie helps Lady Hazel climb inside.

"I'll be back in the morning. For God's sake, keep quiet, or we're all goners." Annie closes the armoire door and leaves the room.

Annie returns to the parlor where Sir John and Lloyd George are taking a break from painting. They are having brandy by the fireplace.

"Lady Hazel has come down with a splitting headache. She has had her driver escort her home, sir. She sends her apologies for her untimely exit, and she said she'd send the driver back for Sir John."

"Oh, what a shame! I do hope she feels better," Lloyd George says to Sir John. The two then finish their drinks and return to being painter and subject.

Later that evening, Lady Hazel dozes off in the armoire. She is awakened by the sound of someone coming down the hall. She notices it is dark and doesn't know how long she's been asleep. Two male voices enter the room. She recognizes one as Lloyd George but doesn't know the other. The men sound drunk and are giggling and bumping off the furniture in the room. The armoire shakes as they bounce off it, landing on the bed. The giggling stops and is replaced by sounds of kissing and clumsy undressing. Hazel is petrified, frozen with fear of being discovered. She feels her heart racing, thinking the two intruders might somehow hear it. She steadies herself with short, deliberate breaths. Outside, she hears moaning and panting, what she knows are sounds of intimacy. She steels herself to kneel so that she can see out the pane of beveled glass. It's Lloyd George and the Duke of Gloucester in the heat of passion. At first, she is so shocked that she inhales deeply. Then, regaining her composure, she reaches for the Kodak and clicks away.

Hazel takes all the photos on the roll of film. Then she quietly settles her head on her purse against the dividing wall inside the armoire. She listens to the sound of the lovemaking for what feels like hours. Eventually, it grows quiet, and she hears someone leave the room. The rest of the night, all she hears is snoring, which she assumes is Lloyd George. She dozes off in little spells throughout the night but is never fully asleep.

Annie Malone enters the room at daybreak. Lloyd George has just finished putting on his robe.

"Sir, your breakfast is ready downstairs. Shall I have it brought up?" she asks.

"No, I shall eat in the parlor this morning, Annie. Thank you," he says while looking out the window. "Why can't all the Irish be as sweet as you?" Annie feigns a smile to hide the contempt she feels in her heart.

"I'll alert the cook to your wishes, sir." Annie leaves the room and heads toward the servants' staircase. Once there, she waits at the top of the stairs. Lloyd George exits the room soon afterward, going downstairs to the parlor by the grand stair. Annie quickly doubles back to the bedroom. Opening the armoire door, she finds Lady Hazel dozed off. When Annie gently shakes her, Lady Hazel awakes with a start.

"Ssshhh!" Annie says with her hand over Lady Hazel's mouth. "Quickly! We must go!" Annie helps Lady Hazel out of the armoire. Hazel stands and stretches; her shoulders and neck are cramped from the night's cozy accommodations. She grabs her shoes and purse from the armoire, ensuring the Kodak is with her. Together, they hustle toward the servants' staircase.

Once in the kitchen, Annie hurries Lady Hazel out the delivery door. Outside, a milk lorry driver helps her into the back of the lorry. Lady Hazel sits between the milk cans in the rear of the truck. The driver, Terrence McNally, is sweet on Annie. She tells him that the woman he is carrying is a flapper Lloyd George had spent the night with and that she must be discreetly carried away from the premises. The smitten Terrence asks no questions and does as Annie asks.

The truck rumbles away from Downing Street. Lady Hazel gets off at Terrence's next delivery stop. She walks a few blocks and hails a cab home in the early morning hours.

The following day, Lady Hazel leaves the residence early in the morning before Sir John awakens. They have separate bedrooms, so he doesn't notice her leaving. They share an understanding in their marriage: he doesn't pay much attention to her comings and goings, and she doesn't need to fabricate lies to explain herself. On this day, she is headed for Johnson Brothers Bakery Supply on Pettis Street, down by Barn Elms Green. She and Sir John picnicked there when they were courting.

Hazel approaches the bakery supply house. She observes a loading dock around the side of the building. Young Liam Boyle is a carpenter's apprentice there. He fills crates with rolling pins and cutting boards. Hazel stands at the corner of the building, unsure if she has the right place. She tries to look discreet by taking out a cigarette from her purse. Seeing Lady Hazel, Liam calls out, "Beautiful picture of a morning, isn't it, my lady?" Hazel realizes she is in the right place. Liam approaches Lady Hazel, offering her a light.

"Yes, it is at that, boy." She smiles and reaches into her purse to retrieve the film canister. Boyle takes the canister from Lady Hazel and bids her, "Good day, Miss." Lady Hazel hurries away across the street to Barn Elms Green.

Liam returns to his work on the loading dock. Reaching into the pile of rolling pins, he pulls out one with a broken handle. The pin is hollowed out on the inside. Boyle places the film canister inside the cavity and screws the broken handle back on. The damaged pin is placed in a crate bound for Mooney and O'Brien's Bakery, Ballbridge Lane, Dublin, Ireland.

CHAPTER 7
DUBLIN, IRELAND
ONE WEEK LATER

It's a rainy morning. Little Finbar is playing in the gutter behind Mooney and O'Brien's Bakery. The lad sails a tin can in the flow of the water toward the storm drain. At the rear door of the bakery is baker Sean O'Donnell, unpacking a recent shipment of rolling pins from England. O'Donnell is a kind-hearted man. Every morning before opening the bakery, he sets out yesterday's rolls on a table by the rear door. It is not pure coincidence that young Finbar is playing on Ballsbridge Lane in the rain. Every morning, he grabs two rolls, one for himself and one for his ma.

This morning is a little different. O'Donnell comes across a pin with a broken handle. He knows it contains correspondence, just like all the previously broken-handled pins from the bakery supply. He calls out to young Finbar. "Here, boy! An early Christmas present for your ma!" Sean tosses the damaged pin to the lad as Finbar nears. "You keep eating your Ma's cooking, and you'll grow up to be a real big fellow."

There it is: the password. Finbar knows he is to take the damaged pin to the library. With the one roll left in his pocket and the rolling pin under his coat, he sets out for the library in the soft Dublin rain.

CHAPTER 8
BÉAL NA BLÁTH, IRELAND
2023

Dorian gently removes the piece of paper from the bottle with a pair of tweezers. They are at the kitchen table. Mary looks over his shoulder. Dorian places the bottle aside and gingerly begins to unfurl the parchment. Sundance anxiously paces around the table, bewildered at what they are doing. Mary retrieves a bacon weight from the drying rack to hold down the top of the document. Together, they gently unroll the sides. Mary places marble coasters on the opposite corners to hold them flat. It reads:

PROCLAMATION AUGUST 21, 1922
AMENDMENT TO ANGLO-IRISH TREATY

The Irish Free State is a self-governing Dominion within the British Commonwealth, Devoiding the creation of the Boundary known as NORTHERN IRELAND TERRITORIES.

ALL OF ULSTER NOW AND FOREVER SHALL BE UNDER SELF-RULE OF THE IRISH FREE STATE.

ENGLAND REPRESENTATIVE   **IRISH FREE STATE REPRESENTATIVE**

LLOYD GEORGE   *MICHAEL COLLINS*

PRIME MINISTER OF GREAT BRITAIN   GENERAL, IRISH FREE STATE ARMY

"Mary! Are you seeing this?" asks Dorian excitedly. "Does this mean what I think it does?" Mary looks down at the document and reads each word aloud slowly.

"I think it means there is no acknowledgment of Northern Ireland as a separate territory," she calmly states.

"Mary! If this is real, this could be worth a lot of money!" Dorian is still very excited.

"It also means a lot of people on both sides suffered, were killed, or starved themselves to death to make a point that was settled a hundred years ago," Mary adds sadly. "Think of the human cost in suffering."

"Let's see if it is real," Dorian says.

"Slow down, Dorian. Think before you act for once," Mary chides. "This document was hidden in a roadside wall a century ago. How could it have gotten there? And if it is real, there could be consequences we can't foresee yet."

"I'll make a copy and send it to Owen at Princeton. He'll know if it is authentic."

CHAPTER 9
PRINCETON UNIVERSITY, PRINCETON, NEW JERSEY
JUNE 2023

"Okay, Margaret, another school year in the books,"
Professor Owen Doran sighs. Owen is a professor of Irish studies at
Princeton University. "I'll be traveling abroad this summer, to Paris,
Rome, Athens, and Amsterdam, and then home." He is talking to his
assistant, Margaret Meehan.

Professor Doran grew up in Upper Creek, New Jersey,
with Dorian. The two were on the same Little League team. They
did not stay in close touch over the years but followed each other's
lives from afar—most Upper Creek friendships are that way. Owen
is an intellectual, hence becoming a professor, he is also a lifelong
bachelor.

Margaret dotes on Owen, making sure he eats enough, picks
up his laundry, and so on.

"Margaret, just save all my mail at the university. No need to
forward any of it. I do not expect anything to be pressing. I will tend
to it all in September when I return."

CHAPTER 10
BÉAL NA BLÁTH, IRELAND
JULY 4, 2023

Dorian brings in the mail. Mary sits at the kitchen table, reading about gardening. Sundance basks in the sunlight coming through the kitchen window.

"It's been two weeks since I mailed Owen that letter. No response," Dorian says, visibly annoyed.

"Maybe he is busy or away. It's not like you keep in touch with him often," Mary responds.

Dorian paces around the kitchen. "I'm not waiting around. Make me another copy of the document," he snaps at Mary. "I'll ride up to Trinity College in Dublin. Somebody there will surely be able to help me."

"Yeah, sure," Mary says dismissively, not looking up from her gardening book.

CHAPTER 11
TRINITY COLLEGE, DUBLIN
JULY 6, 2023

Dorian is up bright and early. He drives to Dublin in the soft summer rain, looking out at the fields full of flocks of sheep with arrays of paint color patterns sprayed on their necks.

"Must be an untrustworthy lot, these shepherds, to have to go through such great lengths to prevent acquirement," he says aloud.

When he finally arrives at Trinity College, he parks the car and carries the copy in a folder under his arm. The rain subsides as he enters the Arts Building. Inside, he walks to the directory of names and room numbers.

"Here it is," he says to himself. "Professor Plumb, room 219." Dorian heads for the stairs, chuckling. "Should say 'in the parlor with the knife!'" He has been cracking himself up this morning; Mary is missing out!

Dorian gains his composure before knocking and entering the office. "Thank you for meeting with me, Professor Plumb," he says with a smirk. "Did you know there is an American board game with a character named Professor Plum?"

"Yes, so I've heard," says Plumb dryly.

"Your accent is British, not Irish," Dorian says inquisitively.

"Very keen of you to notice, Mr. Rinn. It seems Trinity College is an equal opportunity employer," Plumb says condescendingly.

Dorian's back is up. He keeps his cool, though. He had asked for this meeting, but when he did, he didn't expect the professor to be such an ass.

"You asked to meet with me, Mr. Rinn, regarding a letter you've found," Plumb is losing his patience.

"Well, you see, professor, I found this document on my property in Béal na Bláth." Dorian takes out the folder and opens it on Plumb's large mahogany desk. Plumb spins the folder around so it is right side up for him to read.

After about thirty seconds, Plumb looks up and sternly states, "This is a fabrication, a deliberate hoax, or some sort of April Fool's prank." He adds, "It's not worth any money, if that is what you're wondering, Mr. Rinn."

Dejected, Dorian apologizes. "I'm sorry for wasting your time, not to mention Professor Doran's time."

"Excuse me, Mr. Rinn," Professor Plumb gets up to show Dorian out. "Who's Professor Doran?"

"Before I came here, I mailed it to Professor Doran at Princeton University," Dorian says in a namedropping way.

"May I ask what his findings were?" Plumb asks curiously.

Dorian, seeing an opening in this verbal sparring match, says, "I don't know. I haven't heard back from him yet. Not to worry, though. He will see right through it like you did. After all, it *is* Princeton University." Feeling that he had delivered a solid blow, Dorian rises to leave. "Thank you for taking the time to see me, Professor Plumb." Chuckling, Dorian shakes hands and leaves.

Professor Plumb watches Dorian descend the stairs. He quickly turns and goes to his desk, reaches for the phone, and dials MI5.

"Put me through to C. It is Plumb at Trinity College, Dublin."

"One moment," answers the voice on the other end of the

line.

"Yes, hello C, Plumb here. Sir? I think we may have a problem. It seems the Lloyd George Amendment has finally surfaced," Plumb states excitedly.

"I see. Meet me in the library by the Book of Kells exhibit at 4:15 this afternoon," C says as he hangs up the phone.

LATER THAT AFTERNOON AT THE LIBRARY

Professor Plumb is mulling around, reading the information blocks on the tapestries at the Book of Kells exhibit. There are still a few people in the room. The security guard walks from group to group, whispering, "Library closes at 5:00 p.m. Fifteen minutes to closing." He approaches Professor Plumb and is about to give his mantra. "Oh, Professor Plumb, stay as long as you please, sir. I'll just be closing the other areas first." Nodding, he walks away from Plumb.

C steps out from behind a column just after the guard has left. "Who knows? And where is it?" he questions Plumb matter-of-factly.

"An American named Dorian Rinn brought a copy to me today. He says he found it on his property in Béal na Bláth," explains Plumb.

"And?" C asks impatiently.

"I dismissed it as an April Fool's prank of no worth whatsoever," nervously replies Plumb.

"This Rinn, he's satisfied with that?" C asks coldly.

"Yes, Rinn comes off as a brutish clod. He bought it hook, line, and sinker." Plumb regains his confidence.

"Well, what is the problem then?" C grows more impatient.

"It seems Rinn mailed the original to a professor, Owen Doran, at Princeton University. Doran is a professor of Irish studies.

29

And, sir, he is no brutish clod."

"When?"

"He put it in the post a week ago but had not received an answer."

"A week ago, and no answer." C stands, thinking. "Okay, let me know if this brutish clod of yours returns." C turns and leaves the library. Professor Plumb exits a few minutes later, still shaken by the interrogation.

CHAPTER 12
MI5 HEADQUARTERS, LONDON
THE NEXT DAY

C sits at his large mahogany desk inside his office atop the Crystal Building overlooking the Thames in London. In front of him lies a dossier on Owen Doran. It contains his passport number and latest travel stamps, as well as his credit card history and bank statements. Mrs. Wittkamp, his secretary, enters the room with an update.

"Mr. Doran has been traveling in Paris, France, since June 30. He is staying at the Hotel Gustav, 34 Rue Viola, room 219."

"Does he have a traveling companion?" questions C.

"Professor Doran checked in alone and is booked to stay until Tuesday, July 8," replies Mrs. Wittkamp.

"Do you have his address in the States?" C fires back.

"Yes, sir, his office is in the Scheide Caldwell House at Princeton University, and his home is at 1450 Washington Road, Princeton, New Jersey."

"Very well, Mrs. Wittkamp. That will be all." C dismisses her. Mrs. Wittkamp turns and leaves the room. C picks up his private telephone and dials X15X15. It is answered on the second ring.

"Yah?" answers a Russian accent.

"Come in. I have an assignment for you," C says into the

receiver.

"I come tomorrow," states the Russian.

"No, immediately! This is time-sensitive!" demands C as he hangs up the phone.

LATER THAT DAY

The café on Roselyn Wall in London is fairly crowded. It is midday; couples are sitting in booths drinking tea. Others are at the high top tables working on their laptops. Sergey Rasoff enters the café and sits in an empty corner booth.

"What'll it be, handsome?" the perky young waitress asks in a Birmingham accent.

"Tea, black," curtly states the Russian.

"Coming right up, love," the waitress says, still trying to be nice.

While waiting for his tea, Sergey reaches his hands under the tabletop. He feels a folder duct-taped to the underside of the table. He puts the folder in his jacket just as the waitress returns with his tea.

"Here you go, love." Smiling, she puts the tea down. Sergey pays for the tea, leaving no tip, and abruptly leaves the café with the folder. "Bloody Russian cheapskates!" the waitress says aloud to herself.

Sergey Rasoff is a Russian mercenary. He had been with the Wagner Group in Ukraine. After their leader, Yevgeny Prigozhin, was assassinated in a "plane crash," he has been hiring out his services to MI5. In his car, Sergey opens the folder. Inside is a photograph of Owen Doran. Attached to the photo is an address: "Hotel Gustav, Paris, France, room 219." Underneath are the words: "TERMINATE IMMEDIATELY." In a separate envelope in the folder is a fake passport and 10,000 euros.

CHAPTER 13
PARIS, FRANCE
TWO DAYS LATER

It is a beautiful, sunny day. A bright blue sky with large, puffy white clouds is overhead. Owen Doran is eating a croissant while strolling across the Pont De Arts Bridge. He notices all the locks placed there by lovers over the years. Owen stops at the rail and looks out at the River Seine below. As he gazes at the water, his thoughts begin to wander. Owen loves his stay in Paris, the food, the wine, and the beautiful women; maybe he should apply for a position at the Sorbonne, the University of Paris. Owen is tenured at Princeton, but he feels the itch for change. This itch comes over him every couple of years. He has always acted upon it in the past, which is why he is a lifelong bachelor. Owen's thoughts are interrupted by a man who approaches him from behind.

"Do you have the time?" asks the intruder with a thick Russian accent. He carries a closed umbrella in his left hand. Doran turns and looks at his watch, thinking, *What a strange thing to have on such a beautiful day.* He feels a sharp pinch in the side of his calf.

"One forty-five," Owen answers, but the Russian is already walking away. Owen shrugs in bewilderment. He starts to walk to the center of the bridge but suddenly drops to his knees and rolls on his back.

Looking up, Owen watches the clouds roll by against the blue-sky backdrop as life weeps from his eyes. He is dead.

CHAPTER 14
THE LIBRARY, DUBLIN
1922

Emmett Dalton is a handsome twenty-two-year-old, sweet on the librarian Moira O'Donahue. Moira is nineteen years old, bright and pretty, with long red hair. She likes Emmett, but knowing he is one of Collins's Apostles excites and frightens her.

The two had met some years earlier. Moira was riding a tram to school one morning when two British soldiers watched her board the tram and proceeded to harass her. They made Moira empty her school bag of books and were about to search her purse when Emmet came to her aid.

Emmett approached the two soldiers and berated them for picking on a schoolgirl. The two soldiers left Moira alone and proceeded to rough up Emmett, one holding him while the other hit him in the stomach and mouth. The tram driver stopped the tram over the ruckus, and the soldiers departed, leaving Emmett doubled over the seats. Moira was visibly shaken and crying. Regaining his composure, Emmett helped her put her books back in the bag and escorted her to the school gate that morning. Soon after this incident, Emmett approached his friend Vinny Byrne about joining Collins's squad.

Emmett approaches the desk. "A book of poems by Oscar

Wilde, please." Moira smiles and walks to the rolling wooden ladder behind the desk. Emmett admires her figure as she ascends the ladder. Moira returns with the book. Aware that he was watching her, she decided to have a little fun with the handsome Emmett.

"What passage of Mr. Wilde's do you like best?" She sounds coy.

"The one that states, 'Women are meant to be loved, not understood,'" he quickly replies to the challenge. Moira, impressed and blushing, hands him the book. Emmett smiles and turns to leave.

"Mine is 'If you are not too long, I will wait here for you forever,'" Moira whispers to herself as Emmett exits the library.

CHAPTER 15
BÉAL NA BLÁTH, IRELAND
2023

The phone rings in the kitchen. Mary is at the window drinking tea. She is watching Dorian play with Sundance in the front yard. Mary picks up the phone.

"Hello?"

Dorian comes in from outside with the dog. He's about to get some lemonade from the refrigerator.

"Yes, hold on, Fitz. He's right here." Mary gestures to Dorian to get the phone.

"Fitz?" wonders Dorian. William FitzSimmons is Dorian's childhood best friend. Together, they would pitch pennies with their school milk money, and the winner would buy Reese's Peanut Butter Cups, and they each would have one. They were inseparable until about twelve when Fitz moved away. They stay in touch the Upper Creek way, following the details of each other's lives.

Fitz became an FBI agent, making his way up to Regional Chief of the DC area. He retired and is now living on a well-deserved pension—and is an enthusiast of all things Irish.

Dorian takes the phone. "Hello, Fitz, what's up?"

"Bad news, I'm afraid," says Fitz. "Owen Doran's dead."

"What? How?" Dorian looks at Mary. She comes over to

share the receiver.

"He died three days ago in Paris, a heart attack. His mom had his body flown home. She asked me to get a hold of you so we could be pallbearers," says Fitz.

"Christ, Fitz, that's terrible. I haven't seen Owen in years, but if that's what his mom wants, will do. Mary will make the reservations tonight," says Dorian.

"I'll pick you up in Newark. You can stay at my house in Spring Lake. My dad is living with me now. He'd love to see you. Let me know when you have an itinerary."

"Okay, Fitz, I'll be in touch. Goodnight." Dorian hangs up the phone.

Mary tells Dorian, "You go. I told Grace I would take Sundance up so she could see him. I want to ensure she's settled with the new job."

Dorian thinks, *Plumb was right. Ireland is an equal opportunity employer.*

CHAPTER 16
COURT STREET HEADQUARTERS DUBLIN
DECEMBER 1920

Vinny Byrne walks Emmett Dalton up the narrow wooden staircase of the Court Street Headquarters. Inside the office, sitting at a wooden table, is Michael Collins. The two men enter the room.

"Mick, this is Emmett Dalton, the fella I was telling you about," Vinny Byrne says.

"Hello, Emmett, I'm Michael Collins. Pleased to make your acquaintance." Michael Collins stands, and the two men shake hands.

"Likewise," says Emmett, smiling nervously despite his fat lip.

"What happened there?" inquired Collins, touching his lip.

"A little rub with two British soldiers on the tram to Ballsbridge the other morning," Emmett replies, still a little nervous about meeting the Big Fellow.

"So, you come to us for a little revenge, is that it?" Micheal Collins is about to dismiss him from the interview.

"No, sir, not just that. I'm sick of it. Them having their way with our property, our girls, our land. Revenge, yes, but not for a bloody lip. I just want to have a go at them. Can you understand that, Mr. Collins, sir?" Emmett's not nervous anymore; he speaks from the heart.

"This is rough stuff we are engaged in, boy, not just fisticuffs. You understand that, right?" Michael Collins says sternly, looking Emmett right in the eye with his icy stare.

"Yes, sir, I know, and I'm not afraid. As I said, I just want to have a go at them." Emmett looks straight at Collins, then glances over to Vinny Byrne.

"Mick, he's a good, tough lad. I've known him all my life." Vinny wants to convince Collins.

"Okay, we'll give you a shot." Michael Collins shakes Emmett's hand. "You say you ride the Ballsbridge tram?"

"Yes, sir, I work in a bicycle shop in Ringsend," answers Emmett.

Michael Collins gets up from the table and goes into the other room.

Emmett looks at Vinny, shrugs his shoulders, and wonders what is happening. Vinny just smirks and shrugs back. Michael Collins reenters the room with a small photograph in his hands. He hands the photo to Emmett.

"Have you ever seen this man on the tram?" asks Collins sternly.

Emmet looks at the photo, and then up at Collins. "He looks familiar. I think so," Emmett replies.

"Tomorrow, Vinny will meet you at your stop, and you will ride the tram to Ringsend. If you see this man, just let Vinny know," Michael Collins instructs the two men.

"Do I get a gun?" asks Emmett.

"In due time, lad," Collins says. "For now, just point the fellow in the photograph out to Vinny. Understood?".

That evening, Emmett stops by Moira's house.

"I brought you a bicycle. Someone returned it to the shop." Emmett rings the bell on the handlebars with his thumb. "My boss said I could have it. It pedals easily. I lubricated the chain." Emmett is starting to feel awkward.

"Oh, you shouldn't have," says Moira, blushing. "That is so nice of you!"

"Look, it has a basket for your books, so you don't have to ride the tram," Emmett reveals his real reason for gifting the bike to Moira. Emmett had purchased the bicycle himself.

"But then I won't get to see you," blurts out Moira without thinking, blushing soon afterward.

"I'll be around, don't you worry," Emmett says, feeling elated inside that she likes him too.

The next morning, Emmett waits for the tram. Vinny Byrne strolls up, eating a brown bread and rasher sandwich.

"Are you ready, Emmett?" Vinny says, chewing.

"What are we going to do?" Emmett asks. He's a little nervous, but Vinny's assault on the brown bread sandwich makes him laugh and calms his nerves.

"We're just going to ride the tram. I'm going to sit a few seats behind you. If you see the man, take off your cap." Vinny wipes his fingers on his pant legs. "I'm going to get off before Ringsend. You continue on." The two men board the tram and sit apart from each other by a few rows. Two stops later, Alan Bell, the man in the photograph, boards the tram and sits a row in front of Emmett. Emmett waits for Bell to settle and the tram to move again before he nervously takes his hat off and wipes his brow without looking around. At the next stop, Vinny Byrne exits the tram without incident.

TWO WEEKS LATER

Moira O'Donaghue is pedaling her new bicycle to school. As she passes Ballsbridge station, Moira notices a commotion in the street. Dublin Metro Police, DMP, have the other side of the street cordoned off. There is a body covered in a sheet by the curb. The young girl slows down to look at the scene and then notices that the two soldiers who harassed her on the tram are there. She continues to bicycle to school. The next day, in the *Dublin Independent*, it is reported that Alan Bell, a British magistrate, was dragged off the tram by two men and gunned down by the side of the road in broad daylight.

CHAPTER 17
COURT STREET HEADQUARTERS, DUBLIN
JULY 1922

Emmett walks into headquarters with the Oscar Wilde book. As he opens the door, he finds Vinny Byrne sitting in a chair, leaning against the wall. Byrne is eating a bowl of lamb stew the size of a mixing bowl.

"What's doing?" asks Vinny around a spoonful of stew.

"Just back with the correspondence for the Big Fellow," Emmett states, still awed by Vinny's appetite. "Good God, man! Do you ever stop chewing?" He laughs.

"Feck yew, eejit," says Byrne, but he is smiling.

Just then, the Big Fellow enters the room. Vinny sits up with the chair back on four legs and puts the bowl and spoon down. "Emmett's back from the library with the correspondence."

"Let's have it, then," Collins says. Emmett hands the book over to the Big Fellow. "Stew looks good, Vin."

"Aw, sorry, Mick. There's none left," says Vinny, looking embarrassed.

"Go figure," says Emmett with a smile. Collins laughs and steps into the other room, closing the door. Once out of sight of the men, Michael Collins opens the book. The pages are hollowed out, concealing a canister of film negatives. He opens the canister and removes the negative roll inside. In the corner of the sparsely furnished room is a floor lamp. Collins holds the negative roll up to the light.

"Oh my!" he says. "You are a naughty, peculiar man, Sir Lloyd George!" Collins laughs to himself. "Good job, darlin,'" he adds to Lady Hazel, hundreds of miles away.

CHAPTER 18
CREEKSIDE TAVERN, UPPER CREEK, NEW JERSEY
2023

Dorian and Fitz are at the bar after Owen's wake. The night of a wake in Upper Creek is like the night before Thanksgiving in other towns. All the people who come back to town for the funeral congregate at the Creekside Tavern, drinking, crying, and laughing until closing time. The Creekside Tavern is a little hole-in-the-wall type bar; the only thing missing is sawdust on the floor. It is the main watering hole in Upper Creek. When it is crowded and busy, you could not notice how dog-eared a place it is. The bar is packed. Elizabeth Moran, the bartender, is juggling drinks with both hands. Across the bar, Dorian sees his cousin Rita. He waves her over to where he and Fitz are sitting. They try to talk, but the bar is too crowded, with patrons reaching in to order drinks. Fitz sees a just vacated booth, and the trio swoops in.

"Fitz, you know my cousin, Rita? She lived by the church," Dorian says.

"Yeah, I remember Rita. She could remember everyone's birthday!" Fitz laughs, shaking Rita's hand.

"And she could spell 'Supercalifragilisticexpialidocious' in the third grade," Dorian adds. Rita blushes from all the attention. Fitz goes to the bar to buy the first round.

"I didn't know you were close with Owen," Dorian yells to Rita over the noise.

"I only got to know him recently. I bought the house next to Mrs. Doran. I look in on her occasionally, her being all alone. I came back to Upper Creek when I landed the job as food critic for the *Bergen Evening Record*," Rita explains.

Fitz returns with the drinks. They sit and reminisce. The boys take turns buying rounds until closing. They spend the night on Rita's couch and parlor floor, neither in any condition to drive to Spring Lake.

CHAPTER 19
MADONNA CEMETERY, FORT LEE, NEW JERSEY
JULY 2023

It's lightly drizzling as the mourners walk from the grave. Fitz and Dorian get into Fitz's Mazda on their way to the repast.

"Nice car, Fitz." Dorian shakes off the dampness in the passenger seat.

"Yeah, we still get the lifetime family discount," says Fitz, laughing. Fitz's dad, Big Fitz, is a retired US Marine sergeant. He had served in the late 1950s, during the height of the Cold War. He is a tough, no-nonsense Irishman. You have a valuable and dependable ally if Big Fitz is on your side. If he isn't, you have a big problem. Before he retired, Big Fitz was the head of the Mazda USA operation at the Newark Seaport. Nothing moved in or out without Big Fitz knowing and okaying it.

The repast is held at Roberto's Italian Restaurant in Upper Creek, known for its great food. It is a traditional old-school Italian restaurant with large velvet drapes around the windows and sculptures of naked goddesses flanking the bar. The bagpipers from the funeral seem a little out of place, though. Fitz, Dorian, and Rita are at the bar. Mrs. Doran, Owen's ninety-three-year-old mother, approaches them. She has known them since they were kids and still addresses them as if they were.

"Thank you, boys, for today," she says in her delicate Irish brogue.

"Aw, no problem, Mrs. D.," they say simultaneously.

"You're good boys," she adds. "There's one more thing you can do for me."

"Sure, name it," says Dorian, raising his eyebrows at Fitz and Rita.

"The university contacted me about Owen's belongings. They would like them out of his apartment and office before the school year begins in September," she states matter-of-factly.

"All business, those Ivy League bastards, aren't they?" Dorian sips his vodka and cranberry.

"Yeah, we'll go down tomorrow," Fitz reassures the old woman, shooting a look at Dorian for cursing in front of her.

"Thank you, William." She turns to Rita. "I'm ready to leave now, dear." Rita smiles at the boys and leads Mrs. Doran to the coat check.

CHAPTER 20
PRINCETON, NEW JERSEY
THE SAME DAY

Leaping with his six-foot, four-inch frame, Sergey Rasoff
grabs the ladder rung of the wrought iron fire escape. His body
weight pulls the ladder down to street level. He climbs to the second-
floor landing and pulls the ladder back into its storage position.
Sergey moves to the window, breaks the glass pane, and gains access
to Owen Doran's apartment. Once inside the apartment, the Russian
systematically ransacks the entire contents of the premises. Nothing
is spared; the refrigerator contents are spilled into the sink, pillows
and the sofa are cut open, and stuffing is flung about the floor like a
layer of snow. In the bedroom, drawers are turned upside-down. He
cuts the mattress and box spring down the middle with his K-Bar
knife.

Once satisfied that the document is not there, Sergey goes
to the kitchen and takes the toaster off the countertop. He brings it
into the bathroom, places it on the back of the sink, and plugs it in.
Sergey goes to the bedroom and grabs pages of the books he rifled
through. Returning to the bathroom, he stuffs the pages in the toaster
and depresses the lever. He hustles to the kitchen, grabs the stove
with both hands, and shimmies it away from the wall. With his long,
sinewy arms, the Russian reaches for the gas hose and, with a sharp

tug, rips it from the wall. With the hissing sound of gas filling the room, he hurries out the window and down the fire escape. While driving down Washington Road, he hears the explosion. He turns left onto Route 1 North.

Sergey drives a few miles until he spots a roadside motel. The flashing neon sign out front rotates from "Vacancy" to "In-Room Movies." He pulls in, parks around the back, and walks to the front office.

"I would like room for one night," he says curtly.

The woman behind the counter looks up from *The Maury Povich Show* blaring on the small countertop television. She eyes the big blond Russian seductively. "That's $59.95. Double bed with in-room movies," she says, with an emphasis on "in-room movies."

Sergey puts two one-hundred-dollar bills down on the counter. "And a bottle of vodka," he grunts.

Looking up at the muscular Russian, the woman replies coyly, "I'll see what I can do."

Sergey takes the key and leaves the office. Room 219, the key chain has imprinted on it. He enters the room; it smells of pine cleaner. Going to the bed, he takes the pillowcase off the pillow and leaves the room. Back in the car, he heads south on Route 1 toward Princeton.

Sergey arrives at the Jadwin Gymnasium parking lot. He parks the car and waits for nightfall. At dusk, he takes the pillowcase from the passenger seat and walks toward the building that houses European cultural studies. The main door is open, and he finds his way to Professor Doran's office. With a small flashlight in his mouth, he picks the lock and enters. Shining the flashlight around the room, he strikes pay dirt. Atop Professor Doran's English Chestnut desk is a pile of letters and three packages. Sergey quickly puts the entire collection of letters and packages into the pillowcase and leaves without a trace.

Back at the hotel, Sergey unlocks his room door and dumps

the sack's contents onto the bed. He meticulously goes through every piece of correspondence until he finds a letter postmarked from Béal na Bláth, Ireland. "Ah," he sighs, then immediately texts C. "DONE."

Just as he puts the phone down, there is a knock at the door. Rasoff jumps to his feet, grabbing his 9 mm Glock pistol from his belt. Sergey stays silent, standing alongside the door frame with the Glock. The knocking continues with more aggression. After about a minute, the knocking ceases. Sergey hears footsteps walking away on the sidewalk; they sound like high heels. He peers through the peephole in the door. Sergey spies the woman from the office walking away from the door. A few moments later, Sergey cautiously opens the door. At his feet is a bottle of Ketel One Vodka and two tumbler glasses. Sergey looks both ways down the sidewalk of the rooms. Seeing no one, he retrieves the vodka, closes the door, and settles in for the night.

<h1 style="text-align:center">CHAPTER 21
PRINCETON, NEW JERSEY
THE NEXT DAY</h1>

"Google says we've arrived, Fitz," Dorian says.

"Arrived to what, though?" asks Fitz. He pulls up to a burned-out townhouse complex. Police tape cordons off the area. A patrolman is directing traffic on unusually busy Washington Road. Pulling up to the officer, Fitz rolls down his window and addresses him. "I'm retired from the job, DC FBI. What happened here?"

"Gas explosion. Luckily, no one was home," states the officer as he gestures for Fitz to move along; traffic is backing up. Fitz rolls up the window, visibly annoyed that the beat cop didn't snap to attention at his cornucopia of initials. He pulls away slowly while scanning the scene.

"Kids nowadays. No respect," Dorian says with a smirk.

"Shut up, you!" snaps Fitz.

They drive by the scene slowly. They come to the end of the street and stop at the intersection.

"Something doesn't seem right." Fitz looks at Dorian. "Owen has a heart attack while traveling in Europe, and his house has a gas explosion a day after his funeral? Something's off."

Dorian nods, thinking about Fitz's observation. He is about to tell him about the document when Fitz interrupts his train of

52

thought.

"Let's go to his office. See if we can find out anything there." Fitz turns left onto Nassau Street and proceeds to Alexander Road.

At the Scheide Caldwell House, Margaret Meehan lets the two into Owen's office. Still visibly shaken by Owen's sudden demise, Margaret tells them, "It was a lovely service yesterday. I just can't believe he's gone." She begins to cry. Dorian reaches to console her as Fitz scans the room. Regaining composure, Margaret leaves the room to get some boxes for Owen's belongings. The two men are looking around the office when she returns. "That's strange," she says, putting the boxes down.

"What's strange?" inquires Fitz.

"His mail and packages. I had them on his desk, awaiting his return. They were there two days ago," Margaret explains.

"That is strange," says Fitz. Dorian sees that Fitz has been in FBI mode since they passed Owen's apartment. He scans the room, looking for things that are out of place, yet everything seems to be in order.

"Ms. Meehan, has Owen been working on anything special or confidential you know about?" Fitz asks politely.

"No, not that I can recall." Margaret is bewildered at the question. "Professor Doran had just finished grading finals for his students and was looking forward to his European trip. Nothing out of the ordinary."

While Fitz questions Margaret, Dorian packs the books and photos from Owen's desk. Everything fits into a few boxes. *Not much to show for a career in academia,* Dorian thinks.

They stack the boxes outside the office. Fitz goes to pull up the car. After the boxes are loaded, Fitz decides they should take one more look inside the office to be sure they have not missed anything.

While Ms. Meehan shows them out, Fitz notices the doorjamb has scratch marks. As they walk down the hall, Fitz whispers to Dorian, out of earshot of Margaret, "The room has been

broken into."

On the return ride to Spring Lake, Dorian fills Fitz in on everything that has transpired over the last two weeks.

"So let me get this straight. You told Plumb you had mailed it to Owen, not a copy of it, correct?" Fitz turns off Route 1 North onto Garden State Parkway South.

"Yes, and stop saying 'correct' after everything. You make me feel like I'm on the stand. Plumb told me it was a prank or something," Dorian explains.

"Hardly," states Fitz. "I know my Irish history. Michael Collins, the name on that document, was killed in an ambush in Béal na Bláth in 1922. One hundred years later, you find a document there with his name on it? Some coincidence."

"You mean you think it's for real?" asks Dorian.

"Plumb—you said he was a Brit, correct?" Fitz is still in full investigative mode.

"Yeah," replies Dorian, glaring at Fitz for the "correct." "Why would that matter? Do you think Plumb has anything to do with this? He told me it was worthless, an April Fool's prank." Dorian pauses, then adds, "Do you think it is valuable?"

"Maybe we are looking at this wrong," Fitz says without glancing over, his eyes still on the road. "Maybe this document is valuable—not in a money way but in a historical way."

"What do you mean 'historical way?'" No sooner have the words left his mouth than Dorian recalls what Mary said in the kitchen: "It also means a lot of people on both sides suffered, were killed, or starved themselves to make a point that was settled 100 years ago. Think of the cost of human suffering." He repeats this idea to Fitz.

"So, let's suppose it is real. Who would want it and why?" Fitz inquires.

"Collectors?" answers Dorian, still thinking of the money angle.

"Collectors wouldn't want to kill for it. It's not the Mona Lisa. There's got to be another angle." Fitz is more thinking out loud than speaking to Dorian.

"Hey, you said you knew about this guy Collins in Irish history." Dorian looks over at Fitz.

"Yeah. He started the IRA. Without him, there would be no Ireland." Fitz is still in deep thought. "Wait! That's it!"

"What? The IRA? Christ, I hope we're not mixed up with them!" Dorian says excitedly.

"No! They'd be on our side," Fitz explains. "The document stated no more Northern Ireland. The IRA would be for that."

"Who'd be against it?" asks Dorian, still not following.

"Who would have the most to lose?" Fitz is still thinking out loud. "The British government, BREXIT and all. Ireland is still part of the EU. If this document gets out, it will be more of a case than any for a unified Ireland."

Dorian nods along with Fitz's hypothesis. "Plumb was a Brit. That rat bastard sicced the British government after Owen for this document?"

"MI5, more than likely. They are the British equivalent of the CIA," Fitz explains.

"I know who they are. I read LaCarre novels," Dorian answers. Then, suddenly, Dorian shouts, "Shit! I've got to warn Mary! She has the original back in Béal na Bláth!"

CHAPTER 22
GRAFTON STREET, DUBLIN
MIDNIGHT, APRIL 27, 1922

"Thank you for seeing me in, Johnny boy." Michael Collins enters the camera shoppe on Grafton Street, a few doors down from the Kid's Back Public House, a known haunt for Apostles and Republicans alike. It is a dangerous pub.

"No problem. What the Big Fellow wants, the Big Fellow gets," Johnny Darcy says, smiling. Darcy is a developer's apprentice at the shoppe. When he is not working, he hangs around Kid's Back, listening for any tidbits of info that might help the Apostles. "Mick? Will you let me join the Apostles? Just ask them. They know I can be trusted!" Johnny says eagerly.

"Let's have you turn eighteen first, lad. But hopefully, by then, the Apostles' business won't be necessary any longer. Johnny, I need you to work your magic, boy, on these film negatives. I'll warn you now, they are a bit shocking, to say the least, but I need them to seal the deal for the cause." Michael hands over the film canister to Johnny. He adds, "Be careful with them, lad. Don't ruin them, and keep the original negatives intact."

"I'll do my best, Mick!" Johnny walks toward the dark room.

"Do better than that, boy!" hollers Collins after him.

The Big Fellow sits by the picture window in the darkened

storefront. He watches the comings and goings out of Kid's Back. He also looks for any patrolman walking the beat who might question why anyone is in the camera shoppe at such a late hour. You can't tell which patrolmen are Free-Staters and which are Republicans with de Valera. These, indeed, are dangerous times.

An hour passes before Johnny reappears from the dark room. Pale and shaken up, he hands the photos over to Michael Collins. "My God, Michael! What peculiar doings are in these photographs?" he states.

"I know, lad," sighs Collins. "I know." He takes the photographs and the negatives. "Good work, Johnny. Goodnight." He leaves the shoppe and disappears into the darkness of Grafton Street.

CHAPTER 23
SPRING LAKE, NEW JERSEY
JULY 2023

"Dorian, boy! How the hell are ya?" Big Fitz bellows.

"Good, Mr. Fitz, good," replies Dorian, shaking the elder's hand and getting pulled in for a hug.

"He's not good, Pop," interjects Fitz. "He's in a fix. He's got to get back to Ireland without using his passport, credit cards, or anything that can track him."

"What'd ya do, boy? Rob a bank?" Big Fitz laughs. He's drinking coffee and Baileys at his kitchen table. "Come in, sit down. Have some coffee and tell me what's going on."

The two men take off their coats and sit at the table. Mr. Fitz gets two coffee cups from the oak cabinets in the kitchen. Over coffee and Baileys, they fill the older man in on the situation.

"Did you get a hold of your wife?" Big Fitz inquires. "How is Mary? I always liked that girl."

"Yeah, we stopped, and Billy picked up a burner phone on the way down here. I spoke with her briefly. She's to get Grace and go to Christian's cabin in Switzerland." Dorian rises from the table and puts his cup in the dishwasher.

"I figure we still have a day or two before British Intelligence finds out Owen's was a copy, not the original." Fitz the

younger pours himself some more Baileys. Fitz the elder cleans out the coffee pot.

Big Fitz tells them, "Okay, let's not jump into this too fast, but we can't dilly-dally either."

"We can't do anything on an empty stomach," says the younger Fitz. "I'm starving."

"Okay, order some pizza, and we'll figure this out." Big Fitz hands him the phone.

After three slices and two Guinness, the older Fitz stands up and leaves the room. Fitz and Dorian are still eating and look at each other, bewildered. A few minutes later, Big Fitz reenters the room. "Here's what we are going to do. First, Dorian, leave me your wallet and passport. This way, if you are caught or arrested, it will take some time to identify you."

"Caught or arrested? What am I getting caught or arrested for?" Dorian looks at Billy with astonishment.

"Sneaking out of the country? It's illegal, ya know!" Big Fitz laughs. "Now, just listen. No talking till I'm done. I've got a good friend I left in charge at the port when I retired. Hugh McDermott is a burly Irishman who is a little connected with the Belfast lot. IRA Hugh owes me more than a few favors. There is a ship leaving tomorrow morning. Its first stop is Cork, Ireland, then onto Calais, France. It seems Mazda is a big seller in Europe nowadays. Hugh said you should have no trouble getting on the boat. The port hired a new security firm due to shipping delays from many checkpoints. They only check you entering the port once on the piers; you should have no trouble getting on the ship. No more checkpoints."

Fitz and Dorian listen intently while finishing the last of the pizza and sipping their Guinness.

Big Fitz continues. "Once on board, you can camp in one of the cars below decks. The crew doesn't patrol below decks once the ship is at sea. There is no reason to. Security patrols one final time before leaving the port. Then it's clear sailing till you get to Cork."

"Then what?" Dorian's mouth is agape at the plan.

"I can't map out the whole journey for ya, boy! You're gonna have to think on your feet!" bellows the elder. "Now, get a good night's sleep. At 3:00 a.m., Billy will take you to Port Newark. I've got some coveralls in the cellar. You can take them to get on the ship. You'll blend in like a routine maintenance mechanic; take a toolbox for looks. Ditch them once you get below decks." Heading upstairs, he adds, "Now, clean up this mess," pointing to the pizza boxes and empty Guinness bottles. "I'm going to bed. I'll be up to see you off. Goodnight."

"Goodnight, Pop." Fitz gathers up the Guinness bottles.

"Goodnight, Mr. Fitz, and thank you." Dorian follows with the pizza boxes.

Dorian settles on the couch, but sleep is hard to come by. His mind won't shut off. He keeps thinking of Mary telling him in the kitchen, "Dorian, think before you act for once." He has done some crazy things in the past, but nothing like this that had put their lives in danger. Finally, he drifts off.

"Hey, wake up. It's time to go." Fitz shakes Dorian's shoulder.

"Okay, okay. Wow, it feels like I just shut my eyes," Dorian says, sitting up and rubbing his face groggily.

"My pop went back to bed. He laid out the coveralls and the toolbox by the front door. Pop also said to give you this." Fitz hands Dorian an envelope containing five thousand dollars in one-hundred dollar bills as the latter puts on his sneakers.

"What's this? I can't take this, Fitz." Dorian pushes the envelope back to Fitz.

"You'll need the cash till you get home. Remember, you are leaving your passport and credit cards here. You need to stay off the grid. No transactional records anywhere! Once you get home, you must courier the original document to the Times. The genie will be

out of the bottle when the document sees the light of day. They won't try to silence you anymore. It'll be safe for you to return to your regular life." Fitz stuffs the envelope into Dorian's jacket pocket.

"Yeah, sure. Regular life that never sounded so good." Dorian walks out into the early morning air.

Fitz locks up the house. Together, they enter the Miata and head to Port Newark. It's raining, and there are not many cars are on the Jersey Turnpike. The morning commute hasn't started for the masses yet.

"I got you a backpack from the attic last night." Fitz concentrates on the wet road. Dorian is in a daze, watching the gas lights atop the towers of the refineries dance and flicker in the rain.

"Backpack?" Dorian turns to Fitz.

"I put it in the toolbox. Don't forget to remove it before you dump the box and coveralls. It's got granola bars, water, and Reese's Peanut Butter Cups." Fitz smiles.

"Reese's Peanut Butter Cups? Our favorite! You remembered!" Dorian laughs.

"I also put alcohol wipes and deodorant in there, too." They approach exit 13A, Port Newark.

"Alcohol wipes?" Dorian wonders.

"You might get a little stinky after three days holed up in that ship." Fitz laughs while taking the exit, trying to lighten the mood. They approach the port entrance. "Quick. Get in the backseat, cover-up, and stay low." Dorian unbuckles and climbs over the seat. He lies in the back and covers himself with a throw blanket.

The rain is coming down in sheets when Fitz approaches the guard shack. He holds his FBI shield to the glass without rolling down his window. The TSA officer on duty raises the gate and waves him through. The guard is normally conscientious, but it is pouring, and the badge was real. Fitz thinks as he rolls through, *Hope Al Qaeda doesn't attack on a rainy day.*

"The coast is clear," Fitz says. Dorian gets back into the front seat as they near the Mazda pier.

"What was that all about?" Dorian asks.

"The guard will have seen one man enter and one man leave. No suspicion." Fitz feels like he is back on the job. His years with the Bureau had left him an expert in fine details.

Once on the pier, Fitz announces, "Last stop, ladies' lingerie!" and laughs to ease Dorian's nerves. "Now, remember to walk like you belong but not too enthusiastically. You are going to work," Fitz coaches.

"I got this, Fitz. I've been walking onto construction sites for the past thirty-eight years," Dorian reassures his friend. "This won't be playacting."

Fitz grabs his friend's hand before he exits the car. "Hey, keep your wits, and good luck."

"Fitz? Thanks for everything. Tell your pop he's the best." Dorian winks, smiles, and closes the car door.

Donning the coveralls with the toolbox, Dorian heads toward the gangplank. There are groups of other men headed into the ship. They are walking in groups of two or three, sometimes a solitary person, but all headed in the same direction. Dorian just gives a nod or two if eye contact is made, but no small talk. This is Jersey; "How ya doin'?" means "We don't give a shit how you are doing."

Once aboard, Dorian sees the boat has eight decks. He makes his way to the stairwell and descends to the third level. There, he sees cars are still being shunted around. Ducking back into the stairwell, he descends two more decks lower to the fifth level, which is already full. Dorian strips out of the overalls, grabs the backpack with the supplies, and takes the cash out of the toolbox. None of the cars are locked, which bewilders him for a moment, then he realizes, *Who's gonna steal a car at sea?* The fobs are all wired to the blinker lever. Dorian finds a blue sedan, opens the trunk, and deposits the overalls. He closes the trunk, moves a few aisles, finds a red Miata, and stashes the empty toolbox. Once he accomplishes this, he settles in the back of a roomy sedan. Opening the backpack, he reaches for a peanut butter cup, reclines, and tries to get some sleep.

CHAPTER 24
BÉAL NA BLÁTH, IRELAND
DAYS EARLIER, 2023

"Hello?" Mary answers her cell phone. It's an unknown number calling.

"Mary! It's me," Dorian says urgently.

"Dorian, what's the matter?" she asks.

"Mary, listen to me carefully. Things have gone awry. Collect Grace and the dog. You need to get to a safe place," Dorian says excitedly into the burner phone.

"Stop with your spy shit. I'm busy doing laundry. When are you coming home?" Mary frustratedly says. Dorian is an avid reader of John LaCarre; he loves espionage novels. He is always making up crazy scenarios with Mary and the kids.

"Mary, listen to me! This is not a joke!" Dorian says clearly, hoping she won't think he is crying wolf. "The document we found? It's real! Hide it! Gather up Grace and Sundance and go!" Dorian forcefully conveys into the phone. "I have to go now. I love you. I'll be in touch." The phone goes dead. The conversation takes less than two minutes—no chance of a trace.

In shock and disbelief, Mary tries to wrap her head around what Dorian has just said. Mary puts her cell phone down on the kitchen table. She stands for a long minute, just staring out the

kitchen window. Sundance is up from his bed by the window, circling her feet as if he can sense her anxiousness. Mary still stands there frozen momentarily, her head spinning, recalling everything Dorian had said during the brief call. Sundance starts to bark and whimper, pawing at her calves. Finally, she gathers her thoughts and moves into action. Upstairs in her jewelry box, she grabs the key to the portable safe they keep in the linen closet. Mary opens the safe and extracts ten thousand dollars in one-hundred-dollar bills, the emergency cash they keep in case of another financial crisis like 2008. She grabs her passport and packs an overnight bag. Returning to the kitchen, she grabs the bag of dog food and a water bowl. Mary puts Sundance and the luggage into the front seat of the car. She goes back into the house. Mary purposely leaves behind the pocketbook with her wallet, driver's license, credit cards, and cell phone. She is about to leave when she remembers the document.

Mary retrieves the document, stops, and thinks where to hide it. Going down the basement stairs, she sees the empty wine barrel. She rolls the document up and ties a string around the roll to suspend it in the barrel. She then lowers it into the barrel's bunghole, trapping the string and replacing the bung into the barrel. Mary climbs the stairs to leave when she rethinks her hiding place. Returning to the barrel, she extracts the document and puts it into one of the empty wine bottles Dorian has stacked on the shelves. Mary corks the bottle and hurries upstairs to the parlor. She goes to the fireplace. Kneeling in the hearth, reaching her arm up, she opens the damper flap. Mary gently places the wine bottle atop the damper flap. She leaves the house open and climbs into the driver's seat of their car. Looking in the rearview mirror, she thinks, *All his jerky spy shit came in handy.* Mary backs out of the driveway and heads in the direction of Killarney.

CHAPTER 25
CROW STREET SAFE HOUSE, DUBLIN
EARLY HOURS, JUNE 1922

"Thank you for coming," Michael Collins greets Dave Nelligan, a sergeant in the Royal Irish Constabulary. RIC Nelligan was Collins's eyes and ears in Dublin Castle, the intelligence center of the British during the occupation. One winter night in 1919, Nelligan snuck Michael Collins into the records room at Dublin Castle. The Big Fellow spent the night going through the files, learning who the British were using as informants, or touts, and how the Black and Tans operated.

The Black and Tans, as they are called, are auxiliary troops brought to Ireland by Britain. They are mostly made up of ex-WWI soldiers. The Tans are more of a mercenary group than a police force. They terrorize the Irish population with looting, arson, and brutality, all in the name of keeping the peace.

"Dave, I need you to get this package to Andy Cope as soon as possible." Michael Collins hands Nelligan the package.

Andy Cope is the Irish Liaison to the British Parliament. Cope has been one of the key principals who got England to the bargaining table, along with Collins's Apostles' business with Tans, touts, and other British sympathizers.

"Will do, Mick." Nelligan takes the package and leaves.

DUBLIN CASTLE THE FOLLOWING DAY

It's 7:00 a.m. in Dublin Castle. The RIC policemen are coming in to start their daily shift. Dave Nelligan walks up the wide limestone staircase to the main entrance of the building. He sees Andy Cope at the top of the stairs, about to enter the large oak double doors. Nelligan hustles up the steps.

"Mr. Cope. Top of the morning, sir," pipes Dave Nelligan.

"And the rest of the day to you, Sargeant Nelligan." Andy Cope is preparing to return to London later that day. It's a four-hour boat ride. Cope makes the trip twice a month, coming home to see his family in Dublin. He also makes time to clandestinely meet Collins on those "family visits" back to Dublin.

"My wife made biscuits last night. She had me bring them in today. I wrapped a few especially for you, sir." Nelligan hands him the tin of biscuits. "You can eat them on the boat ride back to London."

"That's very kind of you, Sargeant. Thank your lovely wife for me." Cope takes the biscuit tin and places it in his leather briefcase.

Cope gets in the back of the car. His driver is a pro-treaty RIC policeman. Their route takes them past Trinity College's tranquil, manicured walks and ancient buildings. Then the car drives past the burned-out shell of the Four Courts where, weeks earlier, Collins, with a heavy heart, had his newly formed Free State troops open fire with eighteen-pound cannons on the pro-Republican IRA troops occupying the building. The Four Courts was the seat of justice in Ireland. It was considered the opening salvo of this terrible civil war that Ireland is now engaged in. Such is the dichotomy of Ireland presently: beautiful and calm everyday life alongside terrible brother-against-brother killing and destruction. Ringsend, Dublin Bay, is their destination, where Andy Cope boards his ferry to

London.

Once aboard the vessel, Andy Cope settles in his compartment for the four-hour voyage. He opens the biscuit container, and beneath the biscuits, he discovers a note.

Andy,

Enclosed is top-secret photo evidence. Privately, I would like you to show these photos to Lloyd George, P.M. Convey to the good prime minister that I am in possession of the negatives. Tell him he is encouraged to meet with me in Ireland, ALONE. I will personally guarantee his safety.

M.C.

Andy is chewing on one of the biscuits when he opens the envelope. Upon seeing the photographs, he nearly chokes. "Well, I'll be! Huh!" he mutters to himself. He quickly returns the photos to the envelope and slips it into the lining of his overcoat. Andy finishes the biscuits, puts on his coat, and heads topside. Nonchalantly standing at the rail, he drops the biscuit tin and the shredded note into the Irish Sea.

CHAPTER 26
MI5 HEADQUARTERS, LONDON
2023

C exits the lift and approaches his office. Behind her desk, Mrs. Wittkamp looks up from scrolling on her cell phone as she sees him entering. "Good morning, sir."

"Good morning, Mrs. Wittkamp. How did your grandson's football match go?" C feigns sincerity.

"Oh, very well sir! He scored a goal!" Mrs. Wittkamp says proudly.

"   Splendid!" C hustles toward his office door to end this painful discourse.

"Sir? There is a parcel. It came in the middle of the night. I placed it on your desk." Mrs. Wittkamp returns to formality.

C enters his spacious office overlooking the Thames. While hanging up his coat, Mrs. Wittkamp enters carrying a sterling silver tea set. She places it on the large mahogany desk. "Your morning tea, sir."

"Yes, thank you, Mrs. Wittkamp. That will be all." C takes a seat behind the desk. Mrs. Wittkamp about-faces and quickly leaves the room. Once she has closed the door behind her, C opens the large manila envelope on his desk.

"Shit! Shit! Shit!" he exclaims, immediately noticing the

document is a facsimile. "Fucking Igor!" he mutters. "Ignorant Russian!" C presses the intercom on his desk. "Mrs. Wittkamp! Come in here, please!"

Mrs. Wittkamp immediately enters, visibly shaken by the tone she heard through the intercom. "Is there something wrong with the tea, sir?" she asks sheepishly.

"The tea is fine. Summon Agent Somerville. Inform him it is urgent. Also, Mrs. Wittkamp, have the Intelligence Division run a complete background check on Dorian Rinn. He is a Yank living in Ireland. I need his address, passport, credit card activity, known associates, a full workup." C paces at the window with the facsimile in his hand.

"Yes, sir, right away," Mrs. Wittkamp nervously stammers. "Will that be all?"

"Yes, for now." C heads toward the shredder as Mrs. Wittkamp exits the office. He feeds the facsimile and the envelope it came in into the machine.

A short time later, Mrs. Wittkamp enters the office. "Sir, Special Agent Somerville is currently in Spain. He will be boarding a train leaving Madrid in two hours. Intelligence has brought up the report you requested on Mr. Rinn." She places the dossier on the desk in front of C. Taking the untouched tea set, she leaves the room.

CHAPTER 27
PORT OF CORK, IRELAND
JULY 2023

Dorian awakens in the back seat. After three days of rocking at sea, he felt the ship had stopped. On the upper decks, cars are being offloaded. He can hear the hum and feel the vibration of their movement. Quickly gathering all the wrappers from his granola bars and Reese's, he puts them in the backpack. Dorian takes his belongings and goes to a car at the end of a row. Men are taking cars in packs of five topside. He throws the backpack on the passenger seat. Checking himself in the rearview mirror, Dorian thinks, *look as if you belong*. With that thought, he pulls down his woolen Irish cap with a jaunty tilt to the right and awaits his turn to follow the caravan.

The parade of vehicles winds their way upward. Once they exit the ship, the cars are parked in rows on the pier. On his way to his parking spot, Dorian notices a bank of Porta-Potties along the route. He parks his car in line with the others. While walking back toward the ship with the other drivers, he turns to the toilets. Once in the potty, Dorian can hear Mr. Fitz: "Think on your feet, boy." Peering out the vented side of the toilet, he views lorry drivers loading the cars, eight to a carrier. Quickly, he counts out the cars in sets of eight. He exits the toilets and ducks down an aisle to

70

be loaded. Staying low, Dorian opens the driver's door and pops the trunk latch. Making his way around the vehicle, he tosses his backpack in and climbs inside the trunk. Dorian closes the trunk hood, being careful not to let it latch. Soon, he feels the vehicle moving and the bump of the tires rolling up the ramp. If his math is correct, it should be the last car on the bottom row of the lorry. The engine is shut off in the vehicle. Dorian can hear the drivers shouting at each other in Irish. A few minutes later, he feels a lurch forward. The lorry is leaving the Port of Cork.

So far, so good, he thinks.

CHAPTER 28
MI5 HEADQUARTERS, LONDON
2023

C sits at his desk reviewing Dorian Rinn's dossier.

"Excuse me, sir? Special Agent Somerville is here," Mrs. Wittkamp announces over the intercom.

"Show him in," C says loudly enough that no intercom is necessary.

Special Agent Donald Somerville is a veteran Intelligence officer with fifteen years of experience. Before his Intelligence service, Somerville was a British paratrooper in Afghanistan. He is a redhead with an athletic build. Somerville enters the room and closes the door behind him.

"Special Agent Donald Somerville is reporting, sir." Somerville stands in front of C's desk and gives a sharp salute.

"Yes, Somerville, good to see you. Sit down." C is seemingly annoyed at Somerville's formality. "An American, Dorian Rinn, has come into possession of a very important document. This document cannot see the light of day. Understood?" Not waiting for a reply, C continues.

"Rinn's passport stamp informs us he has been back in the States since last week. He has not yet returned to Ireland. His last credit card transaction was at the Creekside Tavern in Upper Creek,

New Jersey. That was five days ago."

"That seems like a long time for the average bloke to go dark." Somerville crossed his legs, getting comfortable in the large leather-backed chair. "Do you suppose he knows we are looking for him, sir?"

"Perhaps." C nods, hands folded in front of him on the desk. "Not exactly sure what he knows or doesn't know. An interaction with another agent led to the assessment Rinn is a bit obtuse, but I'm starting to think that may have been a ruse."

"So, we aren't sure if he has connected the dots or is just oblivious and lucky," Somerville restates what C has already established. C is trying to keep his temper and hands Somerville the dossier.

"I want you to go to Béal na Bláth, Ireland, and search his home, top to bottom."

"Excuse me, sir? You stated Rinn was currently in the States." Somerville sits up, taking the dossier.

"I have another asset running down leads across the pond. You just take care of things at Béal na Bláth." C gestures that it's time for Somerville to leave by standing and walking toward the door. "One more thing, Somerville. Do not be seen!"

"Yes, sir!" Somerville stands and salutes before heading toward the door.

"Yes, yes, very well." C closes the door behind him.

CHAPTER 29
ROUTE 1 MOTEL, NORTH BRUNSWICK, NEW JERSEY
2023

The cell phone buzzing awakens Sergey from his drunken sleep. He covers his head with the pillow, trying to drown out the incessant buzzing. After three consecutive calls, the Russian lifts his head to see who is calling. Immediately, he recognizes the encrypted number.

"Yah?" he grumbles into the phone.

"You're not finished. The document was a fake." C's voice booms into the hungover Russian's ear. "You have a new target. I'm texting you a photo and background info. His last credit card transaction location was Creekside Tavern, Upper Creek, New Jersey. You are to find him and eliminate him." The phone goes dead.

Sergey dresses and takes the empty vodka bottle with him. He wipes the room, puts the key on the nightstand, and closes the door with a handkerchief. The assassin leaves no trace of his ever having been in the motel room. He gets in the car and turns north on Route 1.

Driving up the New Jersey Turnpike, Sergey rolls down the window to throw the vodka bottle in the swamps lining the roadway. The smell of the low tide and the slaughterhouses of Jersey City fills the air. He tosses the bottle and quickly raises the window. "Fucking

New Jersey shithole stinks!" He drives north toward Upper Creek.

CHAPTER 30
BÉAL NA BLÁTH, IRELAND
2023

Special Agent Somerville drives up the winding country lane, occasionally being stopped by herds of sheep blocking the way. Rolling up to a little cottage behind a fieldstone wall, he sees 219 on the mailbox. *This must be the place,* he thinks. The road is too narrow to pull over along the stone wall. Somerville is left with no choice but to pull into the driveway.

He is wearing a Cork County Utilities uniform as he exits the car, clipboard in hand. He grabs an attaché case from the back seat and heads toward the front door. Somerville knocks once, but the door pushes open. Quickly, he glances up and down the road. Seeing no one, he slips inside. Somerville closes the door behind him and slowly enters the kitchen. There, he sees a pocketbook and cell phone on the table. Somerville notices the dog bed below the kitchen window. Reaching into his attaché case, he pulls out a 9 mm Glock pistol with a silencer attached. Systematically, he goes from room to room. Being satisfied that no person or dog is home, Somerville puts the gun in his belt. Drawing the first-floor curtains closed, he proceeds to search the premises extensively.

Somerville opens the refrigerator door. Systematically, he empties the shelves one by one. The kitchen cabinets are emptied in the same fashion. Moving upstairs, the laundry and bedroom dresser drawers are ransacked. In the basement, wine bottles are broken, and the oak barrel is smashed.

After two hours of searching, the special agent is satisfied that the document is not there. Back in the kitchen, Somerville, stepping through the shambles he created, again goes into his attaché case, pulling out a two-liter bottle filled with grain alcohol. At the stove, he empties the teapot onto the floor, then fills it with two liters of grain alcohol. Somerville puts the kettle on the stovetop, ignites the burner, and quickly exits the house. He is driving away when he sees flames erupting from the kitchen windows in the rearview mirror.

CHAPTER 31
PARLIAMENTARY MEETING, LONDON
1922

A roaring fire in the large fireplace takes the chill out of the room. Outside, the rain has been coming down in sheets all day. Prime Minister Lloyd George and his colonial secretary, Winston Churchill, are seated opposite Andy Cope in a conference room in the House of Commons.

"Collins must control this civil unrest in your province." Lloyd George bangs his hand on the table. "Otherwise, it will be considered a breach of the treaty."

"England will have no choice but to send troops back to Ireland to re-establish order if your people cannot," Winston Churchill adds, eager to see the treaty fail.

"No need for that, Mr. Secretary," Andy Cope calmly replies, hiding his disdain for Churchill. "Mr. Collins will have everything under control shortly." The three men rise from the large oak table. While putting on their overcoats to leave, Andy Cope approaches Lloyd George.

"Mr. Prime Minister, sir, would you like to join me for a pint so I can discuss Mr. Collins's ideas on how we should proceed?" he cheerfully suggests, looking like the cat who ate the canary.

I'd rather not drink with you or any Irishman, Mr. Cope,

thinks Lloyd George. Instead, he stiffly replies, "I'm very busy, Mr. Cope." Cope is anticipating this type of response. He has an envelope prepared. While bidding the prime minister "Good day, sir," Cope hands him the envelope.

Lloyd George is bewildered. He takes the envelope and puts it under his overcoat. Descending the House of Commons' wide limestone steps to his waiting car, Lloyd George thinks, *It must be some sort of bribe. The audacity of this Irish fool, thinking he can bribe me, the Prime Minister of Great Britain.*

Once alone at his office at 10 Downing Street, Lloyd George hangs up his overcoat and empties the contents of the envelope on his large mahogany desk. He takes one glance at the photos and instinctively scans the room as if someone else could see them, being fully aware he is alone. There is a note in the envelope along with the photos.

I HAVE THE NEGATIVES. I WILL PUBLISH IN THE NEWSPAPERS UNLESS YOU MEET ME IN IRELAND. COPE WILL FACILITATE MEETING DETAILS. I WILL PERSONALLY GUARANTEE YOUR SAFETY.

Michael Collins

Lloyd George walks to his office door and locks it. He returns to his desk and examines the photos more closely. He is not looking at the subjects of the photo. He scrutinizes the background to see where and how these photographs could have emerged. Lloyd George recognizes his bedroom chamber. The operative must have had access to his home. There must be a spy in Downing Street. So much of the help was Irish. *No, that would be too obvious, even for Collins*, he thought. He'd have to deal with that problem later. Retrieving those negatives was the priority at hand. Lloyd George puts down the photographs and rereads the note.

The leader of an assassination ring guarantees my safety? How comforting, Lloyd George thinks, knowing he has no choice but to meet with Collins and perhaps face scandal, ruin, or assassination.

CHAPTER 32
CREEKSIDE TAVERN, UPPER CREEK, NEW JERSEY
2023

It's around 2:00 p.m. Sergey parks his car along Water Avenue in front of the Creekside Tavern. There are not many cars parked along the road. It's Wednesday, and the lunchtime crowd has left. Sergey walks into the bar and is immediately greeted with the smell of stale beer and urinal cakes. *Fucking New Jersey*, he thinks.

Behind the bar is Elizabeth Moran. She gets up from her seat by the register.

"What can I get ya?" she asks, eyeing up the tall Russian.

"I'm looking for Dorian Rinn. Has he been here? I am an old work friend," Sergey says in his thick Russian accent.

"Oh, you're an electrician, too?" Instinctively, she feels the Russian is lying. Judging from his appearance, the tall Russian in a tracksuit gives her the impression he's not an ironworker. *Looks more like he is here to collect a gambling debt*, she thinks.

"Yes, we work together much." The hungover Russian is losing his patience.

"No, Dorian hasn't been in in months. Do you want a drink? The kitchen is closed," Elizabeth says curtly. The man scares her, but she is putting up a strong front.

The smell of the urinal cakes makes Sergey nauseous.

"Nyet," he says and abruptly leaves.

"Asshole," Elizabeth says under her breath, sighing in relief that her perceived danger is gone. She says aloud to no one, "What trouble has Dorian got himself into now?" Elizabeth had not known him to be a big gambler. *Dorian was known to acquire things occasionally, but how did he get mixed up with the Russian Mob?* she wondered.

Outside in his car, Sergey texts C. "He's been here. The barmaid is lying for him. I'll wait till closing time and interrogate her to find out what she is hiding." He drives away to find a spot to lay low and return for Elizabeth at closing time.

C is sitting at his desk when he receives Sergey's text. He reaches for the intercom on his desk and summons Mrs. Wittkamp. She enters, looking very professional in a new matching pantsuit.

"Mrs. Wittkamp, have Intelligence pull up all credit card receipts for the Creekside Tavern on the night Dorian Rinn was there."

"Yes, sir, straight away," she says, turning to leave.

"Oh, by the way, you look very businesslike this morning, Mrs. Wittkamp." The woman's face beams with appreciation for the compliment. Just as she is about to leave the room, C adds, "I would like a scone with my afternoon tea, please."

"Coming right up, sir." Still blushing like a schoolgirl over the compliment, she closes the large oak door.

A short time later, Mrs. Wittkamp enters with the tea tray and a plate of flavored scones. She places the tray on the edge of the large mahogany desk. C is looking over the credit card receipts. Looking up from the screen, he calls Mrs. Wittkamp as she is turning to leave.

"Mrs. Wittkamp, look at these two receipts here, won't you?" C turns the computer screen at an angle so his secretary can see. Eileen Wittkamp turns back toward the desk. She is elated about

being asked her opinion. She puts on her glasses and leans over the tea set to view the screen. Seeing the awkwardness of her vantage point, C turns the computer screen back and gestures for the woman to come around the desk.

"See here," C points to the screen. "They are identical." Mrs. Wittkamp observes the two receipts in question, noticing each time stamp.

"They're mates, sir. They were taking turns buying rounds. See? Twenty-minute intervals. They were drinking together with a third person. Most likely, it was a woman because three drinks were purchased, and only Mr. Rinn and Mr. William FitzSimmons were buying them." She points to the screen, feeling very important.

"Mrs. Wittkamp, look up William FitzSimmons's address. Dorian Rinn had to be staying somewhere while he was in the States." C turns the computer screen back to its original position, signaling Mrs. Wittkamp was dismissed.

"Oh! Yes, sir, I'll have it right away!" Eileen Wittkamp is thrilled as she heads toward the door.

"Good show, excellent work." C smiles at her as she opens the door.

"Thank you, sir! Thank you!" On her way back to her desk, Mrs. Wittkamp stops in front of the mirror, admiring her pantsuit. *Tonight*, she thinks, *all my plaid skirts are going to the charity shop*. This has been her best day at MI5 in the twenty years she's been working there.

Minutes later, with newfound confidence, Eileen Wittkamp emails C William FitzSimmons's last known mailing address in New Jersey. C immediately texts Sergey, "Forget about interrogating the barmaid and proceed to 219 4th Street, Spring Lake, New Jersey, the residence of William FitzSimmons, Jr. Dorian Rinn may be there."

CHAPTER 34
TRUCKSTOP, IRELAND
NIGHTFALL, 2023

It is getting dark. The lorry driver pulls the car carrier into the truck stop parking lot. He parks the rig under a flickering neon sign that reads "24 HOURS." Dorian senses the vehicle has stopped moving. After the driver departs for the restaurant, Dorian waits until the cover of darkness before exiting the trunk. With his backpack slung over one arm and his Irish cap pulled down over his head, he hurries down the road into the moonless night. He walks for about three hours, not knowing how far he's traveled. Dorian reads a road sign along the way: "Killarney, thirteen kilometers." He feels hungry and exhausted. While walking, Dorian comes upon a historic ring fort. The ancient stone dugouts, remnants of ancient Celtic homesteads, line the Irish countryside. He ducks inside the crude sod and stone structure, out of view from any passing car headlights. The weary traveler lays his head on his backpack and falls asleep.

Dorian awakens before sunrise. He starts walking toward Killarney. In the distance, Dorian can see the lights of downtown Killarney. It's been twelve hours since he finished his last granola bar on the ship. His stomach is growling, and it's affecting his mood. "Hangry," Mary would call it when he got this way.

It is early morning when Dorian enters Killarney.

O'Donoghue's Public House is just opening for the day. Dorian stops in a public restroom, washes off as best he can in the sink, and combs his hair with his fingers. He reaches into the backpack and removes one thousand dollars from the stash, putting the bills in his pocket before returning to the street.

A pretty young waitress seats him at a corner table. When she returns with his coffee and cream, Dorian orders a large Irish breakfast. As the words leave his mouth, he thinks about Mary's comment days earlier about his breakfasts. So much has transpired since then.

Dorian is eating his breakfast of sausage, rashers, eggs, and beans in his machine-like way. He looks up from his meal momentarily. The bartender has turned on the television on the wall behind the bar. RTE1 News reports a terrible house fire in Béal na Bláth. There were no injuries, but the home was destroyed.

"Oh, Christ!" Dorian says aloud. "Mary!" He waves the young waitress over. "My dear, I've lost my cellphone. I will give you seven hundred American dollars to buy yours from you. Please?" Dorian reaches into his pocket, counting out the cash on the table.

"Seven hundred American dollars for me cell?" the girl says excitedly, wondering why he will pay so much. He was a Yank, so probably not IRA, and even if he were, there'd be no trace back to her. She hands Dorian the phone. He gives her eight hundred dollars. "For breakfast and a tip. You're a sweet girl. Thank you." He gets up and leaves O'Donoghue's.

It's turning into a bright, sunny morning in Killarney. Dorian dials Grace's cell phone number. Letting it ring twice, he hangs up. He repeats this pattern three more times. He walks to a park bench in the town square and waits. It is an old trick he and Mary used before cell phones when they were first married. Dorian would call collect from a payphone, ring twice, and hang up. They had only one car back then. Mary knew it would be time to pick him up from the tavern after work. Dorian is just about to try again when the phone

rings. It is Mary on Grace's phone. Knowing the phone may be tapped, she keeps it brief.

"Have seen the news. All safe. Don't let it damper your spirits." Then, she hangs up. She has seen enough Jason Bourne movies with Dorian to know "they" needed time to triangulate locations on cell phones.

Dorian hangs up the phone. While contemplating his next move, he calls a taxi. Once he hangs up, Dorian smashes the phone against the curb and scatters the parts in the nearby stream that runs through the park.

When the taxi arrives, Dorian tells the driver to take him to Béal na Bláth. He hands the driver one of the remaining two one-hundred-dollar bills in his pocket. "No stops along the way, okay?"

"You bet!" says the driver, pocketing the bill. Dorian settles in the backseat for a nap.

CHAPTER 35
MI5 INTELLIGENCE DIVISION
2023

In a room deep underground at MI5 Headquarters, computer analyst Donald Stewart is looking at a grid map of Europe on his monitor. He's been assigned to look for three specific cell numbers. If they pop up, Stewart will immediately notify the Officer of the Day. It's early morning, London time. There has been no action on these numbers in the past three days since he received the assignment. Stewart does not know who the numbers belong to, just to watch for their use. He is drinking his morning tea when, over Switzerland, a cell tower lights up. Matching up the number with the coordinates on a map, he calls the OOD office.

"Sir? It's Analyst Stewart in the observation room, sir."

"Yes, Stewart, what is it?" Officer of the Day David Saunders answers.

"The number three phone, sir, just pinged near Gimmelwald, Switzerland," Stewart nervously informs Saunders.

"Good work, Stewart. I'll notify C immediately." The OOD hangs up the phone.

CHAPTER 36
WESTMINSTER CASTLE, LONDON
1922

It is a bright Sunday morning. Lloyd George's car pulls through the gates of Westminster Castle. He walks to the door and is met by the butler.

"Can I help you, Mr. Prime Minister?"

"Yes, I am here to see the Duke of Gloucester," Lloyd George replies, standing in the entranceway.

"Right this way, sir." The butler leads him through the cavernous foyer and up the grand marble staircase. At the top of the stairs, the two proceed down a long corridor. The butler stops at one of the many large oak doors and knocks. Through the door comes a stern, "Yes?"

"Your Grace? Prime Minister Lloyd George is here to see you," the butler replies to the closed door.

"Show him in," the mystery voice responds. The butler opens the door and gestures for Lloyd George to enter the room.

"That will be all, Jacobs." The voice comes from behind a dressing screen. Jacobs bows to Lloyd George and exits the room, shutting the large door behind him.

"Lloyd, what a pleasant surprise! Did you come for a little morning 'tea'?" The Duke of Gloucester steps shirtless from behind the dressing screen. He flaunts his muscular frame as he walks to his desk.

"No, I am afraid not, but it is about that." Lloyd George pulls the photos from his briefcase and hands them to the shirtless Duke. The Duke is panic-stricken as he shuffles through the photos.

"How could this happen? Who took these photos? Who else has seen them? Are you trying to blackmail me, Lloyd?" The Duke drops the photos on the desk and nervously paces around the room.

"No! Don't be ridiculous!" Lloyd George calms the Duke. "I received the photos from Cope yesterday. They were no doubt given to him by Collins. The terrorist wants to meet with me alone in Ireland."

The Duke is sitting at his desk, still examining the photos. "My father, the King, can never get wind of these photographs. Is that understood? The monarchy will be in ruin! Look at what those damn Bolsheviks did in Russia! You must meet with Collins and come to some sort of agreement. Give him whatever he demands as long as you retrieve and destroy the negatives."

"I'll promise him the world to get the negatives, then quickly take other measures," Lloyd George affirms.

CHAPTER 37
MI5 HEADQUARTERS, LONDON
2023

C sits at his desk. He has just hung up on the phone call from OOD Saunders. Still on speakerphone, he dials Special Agent Somerville.

"Yes, sir, Somerville here," he answers.

"Where are you?" asks C impatiently.

"Staking out the Rinn home in Béal na Bláth," Somerville replies dryly, oblivious to C's annoyance.

"You have already searched it and burned the place to the ground. It is all over the news. What could there be to stake out?" C shouts into the receiver. He is up from his desk, pacing his office.

"I thought Dorian Rinn may return here, sir." Somerville is suddenly well aware of C's disposition.

"Forget that now. Grace Rinn's cell phone has pinged near Gimmelwald, Switzerland. Her mother, Mary, might be there with her. She may have the document in her possession. Rinn's son, Christian, lives in a cabin on the outskirts of Gimmelwald at the foot of Alpine National Park. They may be headed there," C explains, feigning calm.

"Yes, sir." Somerville nods his head as if C can see him.

"Your instructions are to go to Switzerland. If Mary, Grace,

or Christian Rinn have the document in their possession, retrieve it and eliminate any witnesses who may have seen it. Understood?" C emphatically states. .

"But, sir? What of Dorian Rinn? He has surely seen the document," Somerville says, confident he is cluing C in on something he has missed.

"Just get the document and eliminate whoever is there." C is near his boiling point. "Dorian Rinn will be taken as a crackpot or conspiracy theorist for now. He'll most likely meet with an unfortunate accident soon." C hangs up from the call, unable to longer contain his contempt for stupidity. He walks to the window and looks out over the Thames. "This is the aptitude of those who are our empire's last line of defense. God help us!" he says to himself.

CHAPTER 38
SPRING LAKE, NEW JERSEY
2023

It's a quiet Saturday morning down at the shore. Inside the large cedar shake home on 4th Street, Fitz the elder is preparing to watch the Notre Dame versus Army football game. The game is being televised live from Dublin, Ireland. Big Fitz puts the coffee pot on and sets two mugs and a bottle of Baileys on the counter. He expects Billy to return with Taylor ham and egg sandwiches and some Guinness for later on. The game doesn't start for another hour. Big Fitz sits down to watch the pregame pageantry. There is a knock at the front door.

"Who the hell could this be?" he mutters to himself as he rises from the recliner. He isn't expecting anybody unless Billy forgot his keys. Big Fitz walks to the door. Moving the curtain on the glass window, he peers out. At the top of the front steps, he sees a tall, blond man in a tracksuit. Big Fitz opens the door.

"William FitzSimmons?" the tall man questions in a thick Russian accent.

"Yeah? What can I do for you?" Big Fitz answers. With that, Sergey pulls a taser from his jacket pocket. He zaps the elderly man in the neck. Big Fitz collapses in the foyer.

Big Fitz awakens to find himself zip-tied to a kitchen chair.

At the dining room table, the Russian drinks his twelve-year-old Scotch.

"Make yourself at home now, won't ya." Struggling with the ties around his wrists and ankles, Big Fitz adds, "What's this all about?"

Sergey stands over him and asks, "Dorian Rinn? Where is he?"

"Dorian Rinn? I haven't heard that name in years. What's this all about?" Big Fitz says convincingly. His mind is racing. *Is this the bastard who killed Owen?*

Sergey backhands the old man, rocking his head sharply to the right.

"You red bastard! I'd've killed you in my day!" Big Fitz defiantly spits blood from his mouth. "You commie son of a bitch!"

The Russian hits him again.

"Dorian Rinn?" he asks, striking Big Fitz's bloody face for a third time.

"Fuck you, Kruschev!" a battered but unbroken Big Fitz mutters.

The interrogation continues. Big Fitz is losing consciousness but still hasn't answered any of the Russian's questions.

"Hey, Pop! Whose—?" Fitz walks through the door. He stops mid-sentence to process the scene. "Pop!" he yells. Sergey, startled by Billy's entrance, lunges toward him. At that moment, the younger Fitz's training kicks in. He drops the bag of sandwiches, reaches for the 9 mm Glock in his ankle holster, and fires two shots into Sergey's chest just as he is about to grab him. The Russian drops to the floor, blood gurgling from his mouth.

Billy runs to check on his father, grabs a knife from the kitchen counter, and cuts the zip ties. He goes to the house phone and dials 911 for police and an ambulance for his pop. Fitz the elder, regaining his wits, rises from the chair. Shaken but still unbowed, he steps over the dying Russian and stomps a heel into his gurgling

mouth, knocking his front teeth in. "You red bastard!"

Billy hangs up the phone and ushers Big Fitz to the front porch rocker for some air.

"Sit here, Pop, and wait for the ambulance. I'll get you some water and ice for your lip."

Billy walks into the foyer. Looking down at the scene before him, Billy pauses a minute before the police arrive. He spies a small wooden end table across the room. He smashes it and leaves it in the hall near the now-dead Russian.

CHAPTER 39
PARLIAMENT, LONDON, ENGLAND
AUGUST 1922

The session has just closed. While getting his coat to leave, Lloyd George excuses himself from Winston Churchill. "Maybe tomorrow, old chap." Quickly, he leaves the chamber and catches up to Andy Cope while exiting the building.

"Mr. Cope!" Lloyd George calls out. The two men walk beside one another. "I would like to accept your offer for a meeting," Lloyd George adds quietly.

"I thought you would, Mr. Prime Minister," Cope says, smirking. "The Big Fellow has it all planned out," Cope continues as they walk along. "You are to arrive by our boat at Rosscarbery, Ireland. There, you will be escorted by our driver, who will take you to see Collins. Then you can negotiate a compromise."

"Alone?" Lloyd George asks, looking around to see if anyone is watching the two unlikely walking companions.

"Alone!" confirms Cope. "Unless you want to be on the front page of the *London Times*."

"All right," concedes Lloyd George, still nervously scanning the street.

"You are to leave by boat in three days. You will leave St. David's pier at 4:00 p.m. and arrive in Rosscarbery by sunup. Good day, Mr. Prime Minister." Cope crosses the street, leaving Lloyd George standing alone.

CHAPTER 40
10 DOWNING STREET, LONDON
1922

Lloyd George sits at his writing desk, having a glass of Scotch. Opening the drawer, he pulls out some stationery and writes a letter. The recipient is RIC Constable Eugene Igoe, a Protestant Royal Irish Constabulary officer. He worked effectively with the Black and Tans during the Anglo-Irish War before the treaty was signed. Igoe has been a formidable adversary to Collins and his Apostles, though never engaging with them head-to-head. Lloyd George had made his acquaintance some years earlier while inspecting the British troops at Dublin Castle. He had found Igoe tough-minded, courteous, and remarkably handsome. The latter part is what had stuck most in his mind. He writes,

Dear Gene,

I have it on good authority that M. C. will be in County Cork in three days. I would like you to form a welcoming committee for him.
Fondly,

L. G.

Lloyd George seals the envelope with wax. After he finishes his Scotch, Lloyd George summons his valet, Henry. "Please have this delivered by courier tomorrow." He is about to hand him the letter, then rethinks his action. "Never mind, Henry. That will be all." Lloyd George dismisses the valet. He remembers the photos; there is a traitor in his midst. He can trust no one. He will mail the letter himself on the way to parliament in the morning.

It's raining when a special courier arrives at Constable Eugene Igoe's home. Pulling his trench coat collar tightly around his neck, the courier takes his parcel and walks through the front gate. He approaches the cottage's front door. An Irish wolfhound is barking excitedly behind the door. Before the courier knocks, he hears someone command the dog to heel. Igoe opens the door.

"Can I help you?" he asks.

"Special notice, sir, for Constable Eugene Igoe," the courier states nervously, looking behind Igoe for the beast.

"I'm Igoe." Igoe is leaning on the door frame. The courier hands him the envelope, hastily returns to his vehicle, and drives off down the lane in the rain.

Igoe closes the front door. He pours himself a glass of buttermilk and, with the wolfhound lying at his feet, opens the letter. After reading the letter, Igoe puts on his rain slicker and galoshes. He heads out in the rain for the general store a half-mile down the road. The wolfhound trots alongside him in the rain. Upon reaching the store, Igoe and the dog go inside.

"I need to use the telephone," Igoe informs the storekeeper. The storekeeper puts the telephone on the counter. Igoe pauses until the storekeeper leaves him alone. With the wet dog guarding his feet, he telephones his informant in Cork to listen for information on Collin's visit. Denny Long—Denny the Dane, as he is called—is the owner of Long's Tavern. The tavern is located at a crossroads in Cork between Farnes and Béal na Bláth. It is a known meeting place for pro-treaty men. If Collins is coming to Cork, surely someone in Long's Tavern will discuss it.

Hanging up the phone, Igoe and the dog leave, back into the rain, without another word to the shopkeeper.

It's mid-morning. The Big Fellow has summoned Emmett Dalton and Vinny Byrne. Emmett enters the room, panting. "I got here as soon as possible," he says, shaking off the morning drizzle from his overcoat. "I bicycled from the Liffey Bridge in the rain."

Vinny Byrne is already present in a chair with two legs up, leaning back against the wall. "Me, too. I didn't even stop to eat," Byrne chimes in, not knowing he still has egg yolk on his chin, remnants of his Irish breakfast, no doubt.

"You're full of shite!" Emmett laughs as he approaches the wood stove, rubbing his hands together.

Michael Collins enters the room, and both men get serious immediately. Vinny's chair legs hit the floor, and Emmett turns from the stove toward the Big Fellow.

"Boys, we've got some important work ahead of us these next few days," Collins states matter-of-factly. Collins turns to Vinny, seated at the table. "I need you to acquire a delivery truck and be in Rosscarbery in the morning the day after tomorrow." Vinny silently counts the "day after tomorrow, morning" on his fingers. Collins continues, "There, you will pick up a package and deliver it to the safe house at Farnes Crossroads. Understood, lad?"

Vinny, nodding yes, repeats, "The day after tomorrow, morning."

Collins smiles and turns to Emmett, who has sat at the table. "Lad, you're going to be my driver. Okay?"

"Okay!" Emmett replies excitedly.

"I'm off to the library." Michael Collins slaps Vinny, who is still seated, on the shoulder. Leaving the room, he looks at Emmett. "I'll give lovely Moira your regards." Smiling, the Big Fellow winks at the blushing Emmett. He bounds down the stairs two at a time to his awaiting bicycle in the street.

CHAPTER 43
WEST CORK, IRELAND
2023

The taxi driver navigates the winding country roads of West Cork. Dorian sits in the back seat, staring out the window at all the flocks of sheep grazing on the hillsides that line the road, noticing all the different colored paint markings on their necks. Dorian thinks about Mary's message. "All safe. Don't let it damper your spirits." It isn't the message he is thinking about but the words. *Don't let it damper your spirits.* That is not Mary's everyday vocabulary.

Dorian has the driver drop him off two miles up the road from his home in case it is being watched or he is being tracked by the last phone call. *Could they track the taxi driver's phone with AI?* Dorian wonders. In all the spy novels he's read, they take precautions about being followed, so he does, too.

As Dorian approaches the property, a sick feeling comes over him. What had he done? Why doesn't he listen to Mary and not jump into things? When would he ever learn? He could have waited for Owen's response. Why did he have to go to Trinity College? Now Owen is dead. Their retirement dream is a burned-out ruin. The British government may be trying to kill them. He has ruined everything!

Getting closer to the house now, the smell of burned wood

and smoke still lingers in the air. The structure is in ashes. The fireplace and chimney are the only things left standing.

Disgusted, Dorian continues to beat himself up inside. Mary couldn't wait to have tea by the fireplace once the weather turned colder. He starts to cry.

The sound of sheep coming up the road snaps Dorian out of the funk; he wipes his eyes.

"Tragedy! Luckily, no one was hurt," shouts the shepherd over the bleating sheep. "Are you goin' to rebuild?"

"Yes! Yes, we are going to rebuild!" Dorian replies to the shepherd, regaining his composure. "We still have each other," Dorian says to himself. He could rebuild the house with the money left in his annuity fund. Dorian resolves that he will rebuild. He will not let Mary's dream die.

As he walks around the rubble, Dorian gazes at the fieldstone wall in the front yard. "That wall started all this. Symmetry." He laughs, chasing away his despair. Dorian starts to think of the document and Mary's message. *All safe. Don't let it damper your spirits.* The document? Did Mary take it? Did the person who destroyed their home have it? Was it destroyed in the fire? These questions race through Dorian's mind. *All safe. Don't let it damper your spirits.* Mary knew the house had burned when she told him about it. Dorian wanders around in the rubble, thinking and muttering, "Damper your spirits." He glances over at the wheelbarrow in the yard. It seems like it is the only thing salvageable. *That,* he thinks, *and the fireplace.*

"The fireplace! Damper your spirits!" Dorian says aloud, making his way over to the hearth. Crouching down and looking up at the flue, Dorian sees the damper is closed. He positions himself deeper into the firebox and reaches up, pushing on the damper latch. In doing this, he hears something rolling around atop the damper flap. Dorian kneels in the firebox, and bending his elbow as far as it will go, he reaches for the damper lid. He feels something there.

"Damper your spirits! Mary, God love you! You're a genius!" Dorian says aloud.

Dorian repositions himself even further into the firebox. He contorts his arm in the most uncomfortable position to retrieve what feels like a bottle. Once the bottle is exposed to the light of day, Dorian can see the document rolled up inside.

Thinking quickly, Dorian knows he has to get away from the property in case it is under surveillance. As he hurries down the road, Dorian thinks about what Fitz said about publicizing the document. But how? Who can he trust?

CHAPTER 44
ST. DAVIDS PIER, WESTERN COAST OF ENGLAND
1922

Lloyd George's driver, Hamilton, pulls the Rolls Royce roadster onto St. David's Pier. Hamilton slides the curtain separating the front from the rear of the car aside. "We've arrived, sir."

Lloyd George stirs in the cool evening air. He reaches into his wallet and pulls out a wad of bills. "Hamilton, I'll be gone for a day or two. Book some lodging in town." Lloyd George hands him the bills, adding, "Oh, Hamilton, discretion is key."

"Yes, as always, sir." Hamilton opens the rear door of the roadster. Lloyd George exits and stands by the edge of the dock. Fishing boats are returning to port with their day's catch.
A figure approaches him from out of the crowd on the dock. "Mr. George, I presume?" the sailor questions in a low voice.

Lloyd George looks around, then nods to the mariner.

"This way, Mr. Prime Minister." The sailor takes Lloyd George by the arm and escorts him down to the water's edge. The smell of salt water and seaweed hangs in the air. There, a tug is idling, smoke puffing from its single stack. The mysterious mariner gestures to Lloyd George to ascend the gangplank then retreats into the hustle and bustle of the pier. Lloyd George looks around the pier one last time before ascending the gangplank. *Is this the last sight of*

England I'll ever see? he thinks. Once aboard the ship, he is greeted by the tug's captain.

"Welcome aboard, Mr. Prime Minister. This way, if you please." The captain leads Lloyd George below decks to a private stateroom. The stateroom has one porthole a few feet above the waterline, a table with a single wooden chair, and a bunk along the interior wall. A pot of hot stew and a bottle of Jameson whiskey are on the table. "Compliments of Mick Collins," says the captain as he leaves, closing the door behind him.

Lloyd George walks to the table, spoons up a bit of the stew, and then decides to pour himself a whiskey instead. He settles on the bunk for the fourteen-hour voyage.

CHAPTER 45
COUNTY GALWAY, IRELAND
AUGUST 20, 1922

It's early morning when Igoe hears the truck coming up the road. The wolfhound is agitated and starts to bark as it runs along the stone wall in front of the house. Igoe comes out of the house. "Sheba! In the house!" he commands the dog. The truck pulls up to the front gate. It is carrying a handful of Ulster Volunteers, a pro-English paramilitary group. Liam Tobin is the driver of the vehicle. Tobin is an ex-Dublin Castle double agent. He has news that Michael Collins will be in West Cork in two days. Igoe gets into the truck's front seat, and it drives off down the road toward West Cork.

Igoe plans to set up an ambush once they devise where Collins will stay in the region. The Ulster Volunteers are dressed as farmers and armed with pistols and single-shot rifles. The plan is to ambush Collins by the roadside, making it look as if the murder was done by pro-de Valera Republicans. As to where to set up the ambush, Igoe knows that Collins is a very popular figure in his home county, Cork. Word of his arrival and whereabouts will spread quickly throughout the countryside. For now, he and his band of assassins have to get into the general vicinity, and the plan will evolve from there.

CHAPTER 46
DUBLIN, IRELAND
AUGUST 21,1921

The rain falls softly on the streets of Dublin. Emmett Dalton pulls the car in front of Vaughn's Hotel. He sits with the car idling, reading *The Nightingale and the Rose* by Oscar Wilde. Michael Collins comes out of the front doors, bounding down the stairs. He climbs into the back seat. "Good morning, lad!"

Emmett puts the book down and stretches his arm across the back of the passenger seat, exposing his .45-caliber Wembly in his shoulder holster. "Top of the morning, Mick." Lying on the floor of the back seat is a Thompson submachine gun with two extra cartridges of bullets.

"What's all this?" questions Collins, gesturing toward the firearms.

"Security, Mick. It's just you and me," says Emmett, putting the car in gear.

"Okay, lad, but let's hope it won't be needed," replies the Big Fellow.

"Better to hope and have than to need and not have." Emmett smiles in the rearview mirror.

"That is true." Collins settles in the back seat. "Are you reading Oscar Wilde again?" He laughs. "How is young Moira at the

Library?"

Blushing, Emmett just smiles, looks straight ahead, and turns the car toward West Cork.

CHAPTER 47
GIMMELWALD, SWITZERLAND
2023

The sun is just rising over the snow-capped Alps. Christian Rinn loads the last of the camping gear in his Subaru. He stands in the back with the hatchback ajar, taking inventory.

"Tent, sleeping bags, food, coffee, water." He lists the vehicle's contents aloud to ensure nothing is forgotten.

"Grace! Let's go!" Mary yells up the stairs to the loft.

"We're all set," says Christian, entering the house. "Come on, Grace! We are always waiting for her," he says, looking at his mother.

"Oh, stop it! Just start the car. We'll lock up and be right down," Mary chides her oldest.

They are going camping in Alpine National Park for a few days—Mary's idea. She wants to get them someplace off the grid until she can figure out their next move. Mary hasn't told them about the document or anything. She is aware of the house fire but hasn't told the children. Their father is in the States for the funeral of an old friend from Upper Creek; that is all the children know. Mary has hidden all the cell phone chargers, so the phones are coincidentally always out of charge.

"Be in the moment!" she admonishes them.

Mary is indeed worried for them and Dorian. She is a master at disguising her concerns; all the children have picked up on is that she is "cranky" at times. Grace comes down the stairs and puts her bag in the back seat. Mary locks up the house and climbs in the front. Together, they drive off toward the Alps.

CHAPTER 48
SPRING LAKE, NEW JERSEY
2023

The Ocean County Coroner's van pulls away from the house with Sergey's body. One of the two responding police officers is on the front porch.

"Okay, Mr. FitzSimmons, that about does it."

"It's a good thing you came home when you did," says his partner to Fitz, stepping out the front door.

"Yeah," says Billy with a nod.

Big Fitz is being loaded into an ambulance. At first, he refuses to go, but Billy convinces him to get checked, and he says he will bring him home after he is done with the police investigation. They are going to take him to Ocean County Hospital for an evaluation. He has been beaten up pretty well. The ambulance leaves the scene soon after the coroner's van.

The officers have written up the incident as a home invasion, robbery attempt, and assault. Billy does all the talking, telling the officers Big Fitz is too shaken up to answer any questions. Billy fails to mention the tying up and subsequent interrogation. Billy makes up the timeline of events. The stranger broke in, overpowering Big Fitz. Just then, he came in and shot the intruder.

"One thing doesn't add up to me, though," comments the

second officer, still standing in the front doorway. He looks where
Big Fitz had been sitting. There is only one partial bloody footprint.
A right heel, to be exact.

"Oh?" asks Fitz with his FBI badge around his neck. "What's
that?"

"His teeth," the officer says, pointing to his front teeth.
"How did his teeth get broken?"

"When the perp fell, he hit the end table," counters Fitz
convincingly, again adjusting the badge around his neck.

"Oh, that's it! The end table," says the cop, nodding
knowingly. "Okay, good day, sir." The patrolman joins his partner,
who is already in the squad car.

CHAPTER 49
BÉAL NA BLÁTH, IRELAND
2023

Dorian walks into town, having just spent the night at an inn on the outskirts. With a good night's sleep and a hot shower behind him, he has a clear head as he strolls. The bottle and document are safely stowed in his backpack.

Once in town, Dorian spies a French bakery opening for the day's business. He can smell the bread and pastries as he approaches the shop. The bell above the door shakes to life as Dorian enters. A cute young brunette comes to the counter.

"Can I help you, sir?" she says in a lovely Irish accent.

"May I have three boules of peasant bread and a *cawfee*?" Dorian requests, trying unsuccessfully to smooth over his Hudson County tone.

Smiling, the girl packages up the bread and instructs Dorian, "Cream and sugars over there," pointing to a table by the door. Dorian only has one-hundred-dollar bills. He gives her one. Looking at the register, the girl only has three twenties in euros for change. Dorian takes only one twenty; turning to leave, he gives the girl a wink and a smile.

Dorian walks to a park bench in the square across from the post office. While sipping his coffee on the bench, Dorian rips two

loaves into crumbs. A murder of crows gathers as he underhands the crumbs onto the cobblestone square. It's early morning, and only a few pedestrians are strolling through the square. Nobody seems to be paying much attention to the man feeding the crows. Dorian hollows out the third loaf, leaving the crust intact. Nonchalantly, he reaches into the backpack beside him on the bench. He pulls out the bottle and casually fills the cavity of the third loaf with the bottle in one motion. Waiting a few minutes, he dusts himself off the remaining crumbs, and with the prize loaf bag in hand, he heads across the street to the post office.

Immediately upon entering the post office, Dorian is greeted by a chipper woman in her fifties. "Hello, love! What can I do for you today?"

"I would like to purchase a box I can send this loaf of bread to the States in." Dorian smiles, holding up the bag as if it were a show-and-tell.

"Why? Have they no bakeries in the States?" says the jovial woman, laughing.

"No, no, it's not that." Dorian smiles. "I have a cousin there who's a food critic. I would like her to try it." Dorian steps to the counter. The happy postal lady hands him a box, but it is too small.

"I've got others in the back. Wait one second." She disappears from behind the counter. Dorian takes advantage of her absence to quickly compose a note and slip it into the bread bag. When the woman returns, she takes the bread bag from Dorian and packs it into the larger box. "I'll mark it FRAGILE and PERISHABLE. We don't want it to arrive as stale crumbs, do we?" She cheerfully seals up the parcel. "What's the address, love?" she adds.

Dorian recites, smiling at the happy lady, "Rita McCarthy, C/O the *Bergen Evening Record*. Hackensack, New Jersey, 07041. Attention: Living and Arts Department." Dorian pays the seven-euro postage fee with the twenty from the bakery. "Keep the change,

love." After watching the woman put the package in the outgoing canvas bin, Dorian walks out into the mid-morning air. The genie is on its way out of the bottle.

CHAPTER 50
ROSSCARBERY, WEST CORK
MORNING, AUGUST 22, 1922

It's 4:00 a.m. when the tug carrying Lloyd George chugs its way into the inlet around Rabbit Island. Fishing boats are lined up along the channel, heading out to the Irish Sea for the day's catch. The tug moors alongside the fishing pier. The sound of gulls and harbor seals fills the pre-dawn air.

At the end of the wharf, Vinny Byrne is waiting in a fish delivery truck. A tugboat crewman hustles Lloyd George ashore. The prime minister is dressed in a large fisherman's overcoat and a woolen cap pulled down over his brow. The two men approach Vinny's truck.

"Morning," says the tugman.

"Morning," says Vinny, chewing on a dark bread and rasher sandwich. The boatman nods at Vinny, smiling about the sandwich.

"Looks good," he says.

"It was," says Vinny, chewing on the last bite. "Where's the package?" He's all business now. The boatman can see Vinny's .45-caliber Wembley in his shoulder holster through his open jacket.

"Here ya go." The boatman pushes Lloyd George up into the passenger seat of the fish truck. "Ya best deliver him quick. The Big Fellow's waiting." Once he closes the passenger door, the boatman

119

hurries away from the truck back to the tug.

Doing a double take, Vinny looks at Lloyd George and is startled. Apostle Vinny Byrne would have delivered the prime minister another way if this had been two years earlier: to his final judgment. Today, though, his orders are to deliver the package to the safe house in Farnes. Vinny always follows orders. No freelancing. That's why Mick Collins trusts him so much. Vinny puts the truck in gear, and the vehicle lurches forward. They head toward Farnes. Not a word is spoken between the driver and passenger during the whole ride.

CHAPTER 51
CROOKSTOWN, WEST CORK
MORNING, AUGUST 22, 1922

The sun rises over the green hills of County Cork. The car carrying Emmett Dalton and Michael Collins arrives at Sean Galvin's house. Galvin commanded one of the Flying Columns in Cork during the Anglo-Irish War. The two men exit the vehicle and walk to the house.

"Mick! What a great surprise!" Sean Galvin says, coming down the walk to greet them.

"Sean! How the hell are ya?" Michael Collins says while giving Galvin a vigorous handshake that turns into a bear hug. "You remember young Emmett here?" Collins gestures toward Emmett in the background.

"Yes! Him and Vinny Byrne around Crow Street." Galvin reaches his hand out in welcome. "Come inside. My wife is just making breakfast. You're just in time." As the men draw closer to the house, the sound of small children is in the air, along with aromas of coffee and rashers.

In the kitchen, Mrs. Galvin sets extra plates and cups on the table. The men sit down to a full Irish breakfast of rashers, eggs, beans, and coffee.

"Poor Vinny," Emmett says as sips his coffee, "missing out

on such a fine meal."

"Not many a meal does young Vinny miss out on," says
Collins. The three men laugh.

While the men are having breakfast, Mrs. Galvin leaves
with the two children, Sean Jr. and Elish, to sell eggs and milk at the
general store. Together, the children put the cargo in the back of the
cart on a bed of hay and climb aboard. Mrs. Galvin "giddyup"'s the
donkey, and away they go in the morning sunshine.

"Are ya staying long, Mick?" Sean asks, rising from the
table.

"We've got some business in Farnes. If it goes right, it'll
settle all this discord with Dev and his group," Collins says, bringing
his plate and cup to the sink.

"Sounds big. You need anything from me?" Galvin clears the
rest of the table.

"No, your hospitality is enough, Sean," Collins explains.
"We need to keep this low-key until it is concluded. Emmett and I
may stop back tonight, and we'll fill you in on all the details."

At the general store, Mrs. Galvin goes inside to receive
credit for the eggs and milk. Sean Jr. and Elish are helping unload the
cart with the shopkeeper's daughter.

"Guess who's breakfasting at my house?" Sean Jr. says,
trying to impress the little redheaded girl.

"Who?" asks the girl, not looking up from counting the eggs.

"Michael Collins hisself!" shouts the young lad.

"Don't you be lying to me, Sean Galvin! You don't know
Michael Collins!"

"Do too! He's having rashers with me da right now!" the boy
says proudly.

Inside the store, the girl's father overhears the conversation.
Finbar O'Malley is an ex-Ulster volunteer. He moved to Cork
because he fell in love with a beautiful redheaded Catholic girl. They

married and moved to Crookstown to be near her family. When the Galvins leave the store, Finbar goes to the phone and dials up the Dane at Long's Tavern.

"Denny? It's Finbar O'Malley. I've just heard M. C. was at the Galvin farm this morning."

"I'll call Igoe," says the Dane and hangs up.

It is mid-morning with a clear blue sky overhead. Eileen McCrane shuts the front door to the thatch-roofed cottage. Emmett Dalton and Michael Collins drive up and park along the fieldstone wall as Eileen walks through the opening.

"Good morning, Eileen," Mick Collins says from the backseat of the car.

"Good morning, Mr. Collins, sir. Everything inside is just as you requested. I'll be leaving you now. Good day." Eileen hurries down the lane away from the cottage, as she has always done when Mr. Collins needs the premises. Michael Collins exits the car and gestures to Emmett to park the car behind the house. He opens the front door to the cottage. Inside, a pot of stew is simmering over a small fire in the fireplace. A couple of chairs, plates, and cutlery are at the table by the window. Michael Collins walks to the fireplace. On the mantel is a Powers Whiskey bottle and a few tumbler glasses.

"Smells good," Emmett says, walking into the cottage.

"Eat up, lad." The Big Fellow gestures toward the fireplace.

"Naw! I'm still full from breakfast." Emmett rubs his stomach. "Poor Vinny's really missing out today!" He laughs.

The two men turn to the window at the sound of a lorry

coming up the road. In the lorry, Vinny Byrne is with his silent passenger. Rounding the bend, Vinny sees the cottage up ahead. He notices the smoke rising from the chimney of the safe house against the clear blue sky. Instinctively, he pulls the lorry around the back of the house, out of view from the road. He parks beside Emmett's car. Vinny exits the lorry and opens the passenger side door.

"After you, Mr. Prime Minister," says Vinny, waving his arm in a wide mocking bow.

Lloyd George enters the cottage first. Inside, he finds Michael Collins seated at the table. Emmett Dalton is crouched at the window, his .45-caliber pistol drawn since hearing the lorry pull in.

"Easy, lad." Collins makes a calming motion with his hands. Turning to Lloyd George, he says, "Mr. Prime Minister, it's good of you to come. Please have a seat." Collins stands and motions to Lloyd George to join him at the table. "Are you hungry?" Collins asks, pouring Lloyd George a whiskey.

"I'm starving!" pipes up Vinny Byrne, then suddenly realizes Collins wasn't talking to him.

"Go ahead, Vinny," says Michael Collins with a laugh. "Help yourself, lad. Don't be shy."

Vinny sheepishly looks to Emmett, who smirks when the Big Fellow adds, "Why don't you good lads fill your plates and take the Powers? Sit out front and keep an eye out so that Mr. George and I aren't disturbed."

Vinny fills two heaping plates, and Emmett tops off Michael Collins's and Lloyd George's tumblers. The two Apostles leave the cottage and picnic on the fieldstone wall, which offers a good view of the road in both directions.

"Now, Mr. George, I believe I have a film negative you are somewhat anxious about," Michael Collins states sarcastically.

"Okay, Mr. Collins! Enough banter!" Lloyd George says across the table. "What is it you want?"

"Why, Ireland, Mr. Prime Minister! All thirty-two counties

of it! That's all we have ever wanted for seven hundred years!" triumphantly answers the Big Fellow.

Lloyd George takes a pull on the whiskey. He is sweating in the August heat.

"I don't have the authority to give you that," bluffs Lloyd George, wiping his brow with a handkerchief.

"Well, that is a shame, Mr. Prime Minister. Tell me, has the Duke of Gloucester paid any attention to recent events in Russia these past few years? The people there seem to have had enough of their royals and their shenanigans. It would be a shame to see that happen to King George and his brood," Michael Collins states in a not-so-veiled threat.

"You wouldn't dare!" Lloyd George smacks his hand on the table, trying to assert some authority in this negotiation.

"Haven't you heard of me?" Collins says. "I've spent the last three years plotting against and assassinating Englishmen, nobles, and their touts. Do you really think mailing a few lascivious photos to the press is beyond my realm of possibility?" Michael Collins stares across the table at Lloyd George. The latter knows he is not bluffing. "Try me, Mr. George, and not only will I publicize these photos, but you will never leave this room to see the scandal that will follow," Mick Collins adds icily.

"Okay! Okay!" stammers Lloyd George. "The crown will give up the province of Northern Ireland. It will be all one Ireland under the same Home Rule Free State as in the previous treaty." Lloyd George wrings his hands with the handkerchief, takes another pull of the whiskey, and then adds, "But you'll have to deal with the Ulsters!"

"Don't you worry about the Ulsters, Mr. Prime Minister. Once British troops leave, the Ulsters will be my problem," Michael Collins assures him.

"Now, where are the negatives? How do I know this is the end of it?" Lloyd George demands, regaining his confidence.

"I'm a man of my word, Mr. Prime Minister. I assure you if I leave with a signed and stamped treaty, you will never hear or see these photos again." Collins picks up his briefcase and opens it on the table. The open briefcase reveals a .45-caliber pistol, a pen, and paper. Michael Collins removes the pen and paper. He slides them across the table to the Prime Minister of Great Britain.

PROCLAMATION AUGUST 21, 1922
AMENDMENT TO ANGLO-IRISH TREATY

The Irish Free State is a self-governing Dominion within the British Commonwealth, Devoiding the creation of the Boundary known as NORTHERN IRELAND TERRITORIES.

ALL OF ULSTER NOW AND FOREVER SHALL BE UNDER SELF-RULE OF THE IRISH FREE STATE.

ENGLAND REPRESENTATIVE   **IRISH FREE STATE REPRESENTATIVE**

LLOYD GEORGE   MICHAEL COLLINS
PRIME MINISTER OF GREAT BRITAIN   GENERAL, IRISH FREE STATE ARMY

The two men sign the document. Lloyd George attaches his official seal and slides it across the table to Collins.

"Now, there is the matter about the negatives, Mr. Collins," Lloyd George inquires.

"Of course, Mr. Prime Minister." Michael Collins reaches into his briefcase; underneath the .45 is an envelope. Upon seeing

Collins reach for what he thinks is the pistol, Lloyd George starts to cry.

"No! No, please!"

Collins smiles and grabs the envelope, handing it to Lloyd George. "A deal is a deal. No treachery here, Mr. Prime Minister."

Lloyd George opens the envelope, withdraws the negatives, and holds them to the light. Reddening in the face, he whispers, "Are these the only ones?"

"Yes," replies Michael Collins. "You have my word."

Lloyd George stands from the table and crosses the room to the fireplace. He places the envelope and the film into the fire. Both men momentarily stand and watch the celluloid melt into the flames.

The document safely in his briefcase, Michael Collins opens the door and calls out, "Lads!"

Emmett and Vinny head back inside. When the two young men enter, Lloyd George is fully composed, showing no sign of the emotional distress he was in moments earlier.

"Vinny, take our friend back to Rosscarbery. Escort him personally onto the tug. Make sure he arrives unmolested," the Big Fellow instructs. "Understood?"

Vinny nods in the affirmative, then looks at Emmett and says goodbye. He goes back to the lorry with Lloyd George. Once in the truck, the two men resume their silent postures for the long ride back.

"Emmett, let's go," says Mick Collins cheerily. "We'll head back to Dublin tonight." As Emmett heads for the car, Michael Collins opens his briefcase, pulls out a blank sheet of paper, and writes, "Thank You, Mrs. McCrane. M. C." On top of the letter, he leaves a fifty-pound note under a whiskey tumbler.

Emmett pulls the car around. Before climbing in the backseat, Michael Collins grabs the Powers bottle that Emmett and Vinny have been sharing out front.

"Emmett, my boy, I feel like celebrating!" The Big Fellow laughs and closes the back door of the car.

It's a bright Tuesday morning. Rita McCarthy heads out of the elevator to her office. Today, her assignment is to review Il Merlino, a new Italian restaurant opening on the Weehawken Waterfront. She is reviewing her notes on her cell phone as she sits at her computer to write.

"Delivery for you, Ms. McCarthy." The office mailman comes through her opened door.

"Oh, thank you, Gerald." Rita looks up from her computer and stands to receive the box. Gerald hands her the package and leaves through the still-opened door. "Have a blessed day!" she hears him say from down the hall. Rita opens her desk drawer and reaches for a pair of scissors. On the package, she sees the PERISHABLE stamp. She immediately thinks, *not another sample from some bakery soliciting a review.* Rita opens the box. There is a note atop a loaf of French bread.

RITA,
INSIDE LOAF OF BREAD IN A BOTTLE IS AN
IMPORTANT DOCUMENT!
PLEASE GET IT TO THE NY TIMES OR OTHER MAJOR
NEWS OUTLET.
VERY IMPORTANT! VERY DANGEROUS! TELL NO ONE!
SORRY, YOU ARE THE ONLY PERSON I CAN TRUST.
YOUR COUSIN,
DORIAN SUPERCALIFRAGILISTICEXPIALIDOCIOUS

Rita does not fully comprehend what she is reading. She gets up, closes the door to her office, and draws the shades. She gently removes the bottle from the loaf of bread and sees the document inside. It appears to be very old and therefore fragile. Not wanting to handle the document and unsure what to do, Rita puts the bottle in her large tote bag. She informs her assistant that she is not feeling well and will be going home. Rita heads for the elevator.

Driving her car out from the underground garage, Rita checks her rearview mirror to ensure she isn't being followed. *Paranoia is setting in!* she thinks. She turns onto Route 80 East toward George Washington Bridge.

CHAPTER 54
BÉAL NA BLÁTH, IRELAND
2023

Strolling down the street after leaving the post office, Dorian feels helpless to do anything. He doesn't have a passport or identification. He can't get a train to Switzerland. He is very worried about Mary and the children. Frustrated and anxious, aimlessly walking, Dorian finds himself in front of the pub he is staying above called An Teach Beag. Dorian reads the sign and can't figure out what it means. He enters the establishment and takes a seat at the bar. The barkeep comes over.

"What'll you have?" the barkeep asks.

"Give me a pint of Kilarney Blond and a ham and cheese sandwich, please," Dorian responds, thinking that frustration and anxiety haven't curbed his appetite. When the barkeep returns with the pint, Dorian asks, "What does 'An Teach Beag' mean?"

"The little house," replies the barkeep. Judging from the man's tone, Dorian figures he has been asked that question a lot.

"Put a translation up if you're so annoyed by questions," Dorian says as the man returns with his sandwich. He catches himself. Frustration and anxiety are making him belligerent. *Best stop at one beer*, he thinks, biting into his lunch.

CHAPTER 55
NEW YORK TIMES BUILDING, NEW YORK CITY
2023

Rita steps out of the opening elevator doors. She can't help but notice the stark difference in the architecture of the two office buildings. The *Record* building in Hackensack is boxy and dark. The offices are closed in by wood-paneled walls. Here at the *Times*, the floor plan is open. The exterior walls are floor-to-ceiling glass. Natural sunlight shines in from all sides here on the thirty-seventh floor. The offices are also glass enclosed to give the feeling of openness and collaboration between colleagues. The differences are as large as the differences in the two cities themselves. One is the Big Apple, and one Billy Joel sings about: "If that's moving up, I'm moving out!"

The doors close behind her, and Rita approaches the receptionist for the floor's desk. "I'm here to see Skylar Moone. My name is Rita McCarthy. I am with the *Bergen Evening Record*." Rita pauses. The receptionist, dressed to the nines, gives Rita the once-over, deciding in her head, *if that's how their reporters dress, it must be a small-town paper.*

"Is he expecting you, Miss McCarthy?" She says it with a noticeable Staten Island accent.

"It's Ms., and he's not, but he will see me if you let him know I'm here," Rita snarkily replies, sensing the younger woman's attitude.

"Mr. Moone? There is an *Ms.* Rita McCarthy to—" Before the receptionist can finish her statement, Skylar Moone is in his office doorway, waving Rita to come. Rita smiles and confidently walks past the receptionist's desk, ending the feminine sparring.

Skylar Moone is the *Times'* food critic. He and Rita have often crossed paths at food shows and restaurant openings. Skylar has feelings for Rita. She knows it but is hesitant to act.

"Hello, Rita! Come in! What brings you across the river?" Skylar says, kissing Rita hello and gesturing for her to enter his office. Rita immediately closes the door behind her, subconsciously feeling the need for secrecy, oblivious that the walls are glass.

"I'm sorry! I didn't know what to do!" Rita blurts out, trying to keep from crying. "I received a package this morning from my cousin in Ireland. He says it could be dangerous! I didn't know what to do!" Rita can't hold back the tears anymore. Skylar steps in and hugs her.

"It's all right," he soothes her. "Let me see what you have there."

Rita breaks from the embrace, her breathing still unsteady. She reaches into her tote bag with "NAMASTE" stenciled on the sides and pulls out the bottle. Skylar takes the bottle from her and places it on his desk. Seeing something inside, he opens the bottle and gently removes its contents. Rita takes the empty bottle, looks around the office, and returns it to her tote bag, not knowing what else to do with it.

Meanwhile, Skylar unfurls the delicate parchment. Together, they weigh down the corners with books he has on his desk. Once they read the document, the two reporters feel they are in possession of something important, but they don't know what that importance is.

"We have to take this upstairs to Chauncey." Skylar puts the document gently into a manila folder. The pair leave the office and head to the elevator. Rita composes herself for the walk past the Staten Islander's gauntlet.

CHAPTER 56
ALPINE NATIONAL PARK, SWITZERLAND
2023

Agent Somerville has been staking out the Rinns' campsite for six days. He is perched on a mountain ledge about a thousand yards above Mary and the children's camp. Somerville has noted their daily habits and devised a plan to eliminate the trio without any suspicion. He looks for repetitive behavior, something predictable that will enable him to set a trap.

Somerville records the Rinns driving together every other day to the village a few miles up the mountain road. Before returning to camp, they wash up in the public restroom and stop in the local bakery for coffee and pastries. The drive to the village is up a winding cliffside road with hairpin turns. Somerville decides to be at the village tomorrow morning to sabotage Christian Rinn's brake lines. Somerville puts away his binoculars and starts to strike his camp. He can stay at the hostel in the village tonight and await the Rinns' arrival in the morning. He thinks, *I must be getting too old for fieldwork.* It wasn't the nights out in the Alpine wilderness he was referring to. After six days of watching this family unit, he no longer sees them as assignments. He finds himself growing fond of them, how the siblings interact, and how Mary watches over them.

Somerville is a career soldier. When he was younger, he had

had relationships—a girl in every port, like the adage about sailors. Now that he is getting older, in the quiet times before sleep comes, he thinks about what might have been if he'd chosen an ordinary life. Usually, he can compartmentalize these feelings and stow them away. But watching the Rinns, something is coming over him these six days. A sort of Stockholm Syndrome, where he is caring about the Rinns.

They are a nice family, he thinks. *Stop! You are a soldier. You have a job to do!* his inner voice chastises him as he finishes breaking down his tent.

The elevator doors open. Skylar Moone busts onto the floor. "Chauncey! Chauncey! You've got to see this!" Skylar waves the manila folder over his head.

Chauncey Davis is an investigative reporter for the Times who covers the European beat. He won a Pulitzer Prize for Journalism for reporting on the Good Friday Peace Accords between Sinn Fein and the Ulsters in the 1990s.

Skylar opens the file on Chauncey's desk. The veteran reporter scans the document and looks at Moone. "Where did you get this?"

"My cousin from Béal na Bláth, Ireland, sent it to me this morning with this note." Rita hands Chauncey Dorian's note.

Chauncey reads the note and looks at Rita. "There is no time to lose! Your cousin, and we, for that matter, could be in serious danger! Once authenticated, the contents of this document will change history and the present map of Europe."

"Bigger than BREXIT?" Skylar asks.

"Yes! Bigger than BREXIT! This could be the equivalent of the Berlin Wall coming down in 1990!" Chauncey looks at Rita again. "By the way, I'm Chauncey Davis." He extends his hand.

"Oh, I'm sorry! In all the excitement—Chauncey, this is Rita McCarthy from the *Bergen Evening Record*," says Skylar.

"It's nice to meet you, Ms. McCarthy. Are you an investigative reporter?" Chauncey is still holding Rita's hand.

"No. Food critic," Rita says sheepishly, looking at Skylar.

"Rita and I are old friends," Skylar adds. Chauncey releases Rita's hand, picking up on Skylar's tone.

Together, the trio goes to the Breaking News Desk and composes a statement to be released immediately.

The morning is bright and cold. Christian Rinn parks his Subaru Outback in the public lot. Grace and Mary head for the ladies' shower with toothbrushes and personal hygiene bags in hand. Alone, Christian walks around the opposite side of the building to the men's shower. Christian thinks about how much cleaner public areas are in Switzerland compared to the States. He strips down and goes under the cascading water.

Outside, Agent Somerville watches the Rinns' arrival. From previous stakeouts, he knows he has between eleven and fifteen minutes before the Rinns finish washing up. They will spend ten to twelve minutes in the bakery before returning to the Subaru. Somerville sets the timer on his wristwatch for fifteen minutes. He reaches across the front seat of his Range Rover and removes a 9 mm Glock pistol with a silencer attached. Putting the pistol on the passenger floor, Somerville goes into the bag again to retrieve a pair of wire cutters. The MI5 operative pulls his car behind the Subaru. Somerville pops the hood of the Range Rover. He gets out with the bolt cutters at his side and bends over the front of the car, appearing to have engine trouble. After a quick 360-degree scan of the area, Somerville lies down, slides under the Subaru, and cuts both rear brake lines. Brake fluid begins to seep around the interior of the rear tires. Quickly, Somerville rises to his feet, shuts the hood, and reverses the Range Rover to a desolate corner of the lot, still maintaining an unobstructed view of the Subaru.

Outside the restrooms, Christian waits for his mother and sister. Mary exits the ladies' room first, followed by Grace, brushing her wet hair while walking.

"What are you hungry for this morning?" Christian walks toward the women. Together, they head in the direction of the bakery.

"I'll just have a coffee and pick at yours," Mary replies.

"How do you know what we're getting?" Grace laughs as the trio enters the bakery.

Just then, Mary gets suddenly sullen. She recalls the conversation about breakfast with Dorian the morning this all started.

"Mom, are you all right? What's wrong? You blanked out on us." Grace shakes her arm gently as the counterperson awaits the order.

"Two scones and three coffees, please," Christian asks the counter person. There is a television behind the bakery counter. Grace is paying for the coffee and scones when she sees a news announcement on the television.

BREAKING NEWS NOW.
A ONE-HUNDRED-YEAR-OLD DOCUMENT
DISSOLVING THE NORTHERN IRELAND BORDER
AND LEGALLY UNIFYING IRELAND HAS
REPORTEDLY BEEN DISCOVERED.
THE BRITISH PARLIAMENT HAS SCHEDULED AN
EMERGENCY SESSION THIS MORNING, AND DÁIL
ÉIREANN IS IN SESSION AS WE SPEAK. STAY TUNED
FOR MORE INFORMATION.

Mary starts to cry uncontrollably. "He's done it! Your

father's done it!" She hugs the bewildered children, still sobbing.

"Mom? Are you okay?" Grace asks, holding her mother at arm's length.

"Yes! Yes! We are all okay now!" Mary smiles at her children, pulling Grace in for a bear hug, still crying.

"Let's go." Christian nods to Grace, still not comprehending the reason for their mother's sudden attack of emotion.

Somerville's phone rings. He is in the corner of the lot, waiting for the Rinns to exit the bakery.

"Yes? Somerville here," he answers, still watching the bakery entrance.

"Where are you?" C barks into the other end of the phone. Somerville recognizes C's voice. He sits up straighter and instinctively answers.

"I'm in Switzerland, sir. The mission is very close to completion."

"Abort mission! I repeat, abort!" exclaims C over the receiver.

"But, sir?" Somerville questions as the Rinns exit the bakery and cross the street to their car.

"Abort mission! No more casualties! It is over!" C is calmer but maintains a stern voice. "Understood?"

"Yes, sir," Somerville acknowledges the order. The Rinns are getting into the Subaru. C hangs up the phone. Agent Somerville quickly drops the phone, reaches for the floor of the passenger seat, and grabs the 9 mm Glock pistol.

Christian Rinn reverses the Subaru, reaches his hand behind his mother in the passenger seat, and starts to back out of the parking spot. Agent Somerville fires two silenced shots, each striking the Subaru's rear tires.

"What was that?" Mary shouts, feeling something shake the compact car. The low air alarm goes off on the dashboard.

"What'd you do now, Christian?" Grace chimes from the

backseat. Christian puts the car in park and gets out to investigate.

"Shit! Shit!" he shouts, seeing the two flats. A car pulls up alongside Mary's window.

"Are you all right? Can I be of assistance?" the man in the Range Rover asks.

Mary immediately notices a British accent. "No, no, we'll be fine, thank you."

"Safe travels to you then, Mary," the Brit says. Mary makes eye contact with Somerville, and a sense of knowing comes over her. Somerville smiles, rolls up the window, and slowly drives away. He thinks, *Did the Rinns just have their Abraham and Isaac moment, or did I? It's time to retire.*

Mary gets visibly shaken as she watches the Range Rover pull out of the parking lot.

"That man! That man!" Mary is finally breaking down. The stress of the last few days is starting to bubble over.

"Mom, it's all right. It's only a couple of flat tires," Christian says as he approaches the passenger side. Christian reaches through the window to console Mary.

"It's all right, Mom. We'll call for service. They'll come to fix it. No need to be upset," Grace says as she rubs her mother's shoulder from the back seat. Mary sits quietly, breathing heavily while she watches the Range Rover drive out of sight.

CHAPTER 59
GALVIN FARM, CROOKSTOWN, IRELAND
EARLY AFTERNOON, AUGUST 22, 1922

Sean Galvin is feeding his cows in the early afternoon sun. Sean Jr. is playing on the fence as his father pitches the hay for the animals. The junior Galvin climbs down from the fence and asks his dad, "I didn't know you knew Michael Collins, Da?"

Sean Galvin stops working and kneels next to his son. "We are old mates. We played hurling together when we were your age."

"Katie O'Malley didn't believe me this morning that he was breakfasting with you," young Sean explains to his father.

"What? When?" Sean Sr. grabs the boy by his shoulders.

"This morning, when we were dropping off the eggs. I said Michael Collins was breakfasting with you, and she called me a liar," Young Sean innocently tells his father, not knowing the consequences of his morning bragging.

"Quick, boy, go tell your ma to take you and Elish to Aunt Minnie's house straight away." The elder Galvin knows of Finbar O'Malley's Ulster background.

Young Sean gets to the house. "Ma, we have to go to Aunt Minnie's, Da says right away."

Elizabeth Galvin stops putting away the morning dishes. She knows that her sister Minnie's farm, across the fields from theirs, is a safe house for them in the event of trouble.

"Why? Did he say why?" she asks her son.

"No, Ma. I told him how Katie O'Malley didn't believe Michael Collins was here."

Everything becomes clear to Elizabeth in an instant. She calls Elish to come down from cleaning the bedrooms. The trio heads out across the backfield toward Aunt Minnie's farm, Elizabeth taking Sean's pistol with them for security.

Out in the field, Sean Galvin is heading toward the barn when a covered lorry pulls up. Immediately, Igoe's men disembark from the lorry and intercept Galvin before he can get to his shotgun in the barn. The men restrain him as Igoe approaches. Galvin recognizes Igoe. Igoe has a reputation for tough, violent interrogations. The Apostles call the interrogation room in Dublin Castle he Knocking Shop"—and Igoe runs it.

"Where is Michael Collins?" Igoe hits Galvin in the jaw before he can answer. Galvin's head rocks to the side. He is being propped up by two of Igoe's goons. Sean Galvin withstands a terrible beating before losing consciousness. He tells Igoe nothing. Igoe's men set fire to the barn. Galvin is left unconscious in the field.

"Come on!" Igoe instructs his men. "Back to the truck!" Before leaving, they unhitch Galvin's donkey and run it off. The men take the cart and tow it behind the truck. Up the road a couple of miles, Igoe finds a good spot for an ambush. He concludes that Collins will come this way on his way back to Dublin. The men exit the lorry. They place the stolen cart in the middle of the road and tip it over to rest on one wheel while the other spins skyward. Igoe and his men take up positions on the right side of the road. There is a grouping of boulders that make a good vantage point to fire on the road below. Denny the Dane drives the empty lorry to Long's Tavern, about a half-mile from the ambush spot toward Farnes. The Dane is to be a lookout and signal the ambush party with a pistol shot at the sight of Collins's car.

CHAPTER 60
BÉAL NA BLÁTH, IRELAND
2023

Dorian sits in his rented room above the pub. He is at the window looking down on the street below. People are filling up the street, coming out of shops. The cars are beeping their horns. Downstairs in the pub, he hears a ruckus. Patrons are cheering, but it doesn't die down as it would if it was over a sporting event. Dorian goes down to investigate. By now, the streets are jammed with people; everybody's cheering. Dorian enters the crowded pub. The television above the bar has everyone's attention. The newscaster on RTE 1 is crying.

Through her tears, she reports, "Today, the *New York Times* is reporting a document has been found signed by Prime Minister Lloyd George and General of the Irish Free State Army Michael Collins, dated August 22, 1922. The document states that the Provisional Border of Northern Ireland is dissolved! All six counties of Ulster are under Irish Rule!" Wiping her tears, she looks squarely into the camera, "A united Ireland at last!"

"Pints all around!" cries the barman. "Pints all around!"

Shouts of "Up the Republic!" and "Hoorah for Michael Collins!" fill the room.

Dorian sits alone in a corner booth. "She's done it! Rita's

pulled through!" he says aloud. "I have to get a hold of Mary."
Dorian waves over the waitress. Reaching into his pocket for more of
Fitz Sr.'s cash, Dorian propositions the girl for her cell phone.

CHAPTER 61
BÉAL NA BLÁTH, IRELAND
AUGUST 22, 1922

It's early evening when Emmett Dalton drives past Long's Tavern on the way back to Dublin. Michael Collins is in the back seat. In front of the tavern, Denny the Dane recognizes Collins's car by the Free State license plate. The Dane watches the car drive by, waits a few seconds, and fires his pistol in the air. The car rounds the bend in the road. Michael Collins hears the shot from the back seat and thinks someone must be rabbit hunting. Up ahead, Emmett sees a two-wheeled cart tipped on its side in the middle of the road. The cart resembles the one Mrs. Galvin was driving earlier that morning. Emmett stops the car a few yards before the cart. He gets out of the car. As Emmett tries to upright the cart, gunfire erupts from the right side of the road.

"Mick! It's an ambush!" exclaims Emmett. He ducks behind the cart and returns fire at the hillside with his .45. Michael Collins is out of the back seat, leaving the car door ajar. He takes cover behind a fieldstone wall. The two men are pinned down by rifle and pistol fire coming from the hill. Michael Collins lets out a burst of bullets from the Thompson submachine gun from behind the wall. The hail of bullets sprays the hillside. Emmett takes advantage of the covering fire and repositions himself behind the stone wall. Collins and

Emmett are forty feet apart behind the fieldstone wall. They return fire at the hillside.

The skirmish ebbs and flows for about fifteen minutes. The Thompson gun jams. Emmett manages to kill two of Igoe's men when they try to rush his position; their bodies are in the road, yards from the cart. Emmett makes his way along the wall to where Michael Collins is by the car.

"Are you hit, Mick?" Emmett shouts.

"No, lad. I'm all right," Collins calmly replies. The two men are low on ammunition. Michael Collins leaps over the wall to the car. Rifle fire from the hillside pings off the hood and roof of the car. He grabs his briefcase from the back seat with the .45-caliber pistol, document, and the Powers Whiskey bottle inside. Emmett fires at the ambushers, allowing the Big Fellow to escape over the wall.

Michael Collins opens the briefcase. He takes out the .45 and divides the ammunition with Emmett.

"They can't get ahold of this," Michael Collins says, pointing to the briefcase containing the recently signed document.

"Okay, Mick!" assures Emmett Dalton. They duck lower as a cascade of bullets strikes the wall.

"They are going to try and flank us," Collins tells his faithful Apostle. Michael Collins hands Emmett the Powers Whiskey bottle. "Here, lad. Finish it."

"To you, Big Fellow!" Emmett tilts the neck of the bottle toward Collins. "I'd follow you to hell if need be!" He swigs down the last of the whiskey.

"Let's hope it doesn't come to that, lad!" Collins laughs. Emmett is about to give the bottle a hurl at the hillside. "No! No! Give it here." Michael Collins stops him mid-toss. He takes the bottle from Emmett. Out of the briefcase, he takes the document, rolls it up, and seals it in the bottle.

There is an uneasy cease-fire coming from the hill. Igoe's men are repositioning. Michael Collins takes advantage of the brief respite. Thinking quickly, he proceeds to hollow out a section of the fieldstone wall. The Big Fellow places the bottle into the cavity and recovers it with stones. Emmett, not understanding, looks on.

"I think these are Lloyd George's operatives," Collins explains. "They are after the document. I'm going to throw the briefcase over the wall. Hopefully, they will think they got what they came for. We'll slip away and retrieve it later."

Just then, Igoe comes around the right, gun blazing. A shot hits Michael Collins behind the right ear. He falls limp.

Emmett turns and recognizes Igoe and shouts, "You've killed him, you bastard!" Emmett fires three shots into Igoe's chest. He rushes to Collin's body. "Mick! Stay with me! Mick!"

Michael Collins is dead.

In a blind rage, Emmett Dalton takes Collins's .45. He leaps over the wall and charges across the road toward the hillside, guns blazing. He routs the ambushers. Denny the Dane is running up the road from Long's Tavern. Seeing Emmett in the middle of the road, he shoots him from behind and flees the scene. Emmett falls to the ground, the wind knocked out of his lungs, rolling onto his back. Blood percolates out of his mouth as he struggles to breathe. The taste of his blood reminds him of the day on the tram when he met Moira. His senses are heightened. There is a burning in his chest and an underwater feeling in his ears. Looking up, he notices the sun setting, and the sky is ablaze with red. Emmett hears Moira quoting Oscar Wilde in his head: "If you are not too long, I'll wait here for you forever." *She didn't think I heard her that day at the library.* His breathing is getting faint. Emmett thinks of Moira's smile as life leaves him.

CHAPTER 62
SWISS ALPS, SWITZERLAND
2023

Grace, Mary, and Christian head down the mountain. They are packed up from camping and heading back to Christian's house in Gimmelwald. Christian's Subaru is getting fixed, and Mary has rented a Mazda CX-5.

It handles nicely on the turns! she thinks.

Grace's cell phone rings twice, then stops. A few seconds later, it rings again. "It's a strange number," Grace says, deleting the call. The phone rings a third time.

"Answer it! Answer it!" Mary exclaims, trying to keep her eyes on the road while she glares at Grace in the rearview mirror.

"Why?" questions Grace.

"Just answer the damn phone!" yells Mary, swerving the car.

"Hello?" says Grace into the phone.

"Grace, honey! It's Dad! It's over!" Dorian says over the receiver. He is shouting over the barroom celebration in the background.

"What's over, Dad?" Grace asks, bewildered.

"Gimme the damn phone!" Mary pulls at Grace's sleeve while keeping one hand on the steering wheel. "Dorian!" Mary finally has the phone.

"Mary! Thank God! Mary! Have you seen the news? It's over! The genie is out of the bottle!" exclaims Dorian. "You can come home!" Dorian starts to cry.

"Home—that word never sounded so good!" Mary tries to keep her emotions in check.

"We'll rebuild." Dorian wipes tears from his eyes. "We can still do it, like in the old days! I'm in Béal na Bláth, staying at An Teach Beag. Don't ask what it means." He laughs.

"We can be there in two days. Are you all right?" Mary asks. Her emotions are finally getting to her.

"Never better, darling," Dorian smiles through the phone. "Never better. It's over!"

CHAPTER 63
SPRING LAKE, NEW JERSEY
2023

Mr. Fitz and Billy are watching Notre Dame versus. USC on television.

"No Anthony Davis shit this year!" Says Mr. Fitz. The swelling in his face is all gone, but he still has remnants of broken blood vessels in the whites of his eye.

"No, not this year, Pop!" Billy smiles. He walks into the kitchen for a sandwich.

Over the television, they hear, "We interrupt this broadcast for a special announcement from *World News Tonight*."

"Ah, shit!" shouts Fitz the elder. "They're on the ten-yard line! What the hell?"

"This is David Muir reporting. A document has surfaced that dissolves the Northern Ireland Border. The British Parliament is in emergency session. The Irish parliament is also in session," reports Muir.

"My God! The boy's done it!" shouts Big Fitz. "Billy! Billy! Look at that! He's done it! Good boy, Dorian! Good boy!"

EPILOGUE
GLASNEVIN CEMETERY, DUBLIN, IRELAND
2023

It's a quiet autumn Sunday morning. Dorian Rinn slowly approaches Michael Collins's grave. He places flowers on the grave, adding them to the existing mound of fresh bouquets. While Dorian quietly says a prayer at the graveside, another man stands nearby.

"They don't make 'em like him anymore," the young stranger states in a thick Irish brogue.

"Yeah, he was somethin'," Dorian replies quietly.

"You're from the States?" The young Irishman notices Dorian's Hudson County accent.

"Dorian Rinn." Dorian extends his arm to shake the Irishman's hand.

"Vinny Byrne III." The young man vigorously shakes Dorian's hand. "My grandfather was one of his Apostles." Byrne nods toward the headstone.

"I would love to hear about it," says Dorian. "Can I buy you breakfast?"

"I'd like that," says Vinny Byrne III with a smile.

THE END

About the Author

Joel Ring resides in New Jersey with his wife and three children. Discovery at Béal na Bláth is his first endeavor in writing.